The Dragon's Mark

by Eclipsa Moon

The Dragon's Mark

by Eclipsa Moon

Published by

ARKETT PUBLISHING
division of Arkettype
PO Box 36, Gaylordsville, CT 06755
806-350-4007 • Fax 860-355-3970
www.local-author.com

ISBN 978-1-0879-3558-4

Printed in USA.

Cover by Arkettype.

Dedicated to

Trinity Mink
Without you, none of this
would be possible

Prologue

In a town with nothing but forest around lived a child. She lived in a house away from the town in the forest. That girl is me. I lived there with my parents who worked in the town. I was a happy baby with long white hair, piercing green eyes and fair skin. I had a happy childhood too. My parents would play in the backyard with me. They would make cartoon characters and my imaginary friends using air illusions or stone figures. My parents were mages and so am I (well once I'm older I will be).

My family is an old mystical family, and I am the last descendant of our family. My parents were the best in their class at school, they had attended it as teens.

The fun and happiness couldn't last though and ended when I was six. I got into a fight with my parents, (I was a very mature child for my age, I started talking at 1½). The argument was about the fact that I could never go into town or anywhere outside of the woods. The woods to me were like a second home since I wasn't allowed anywhere else beside the house. They yelled at me for questioning their decisions and sent me to my room. I was mad at them too, so I slammed the door to my room. I sat grumpily on my bed.

"Why can't I go past the woods" I thought? I let out a yawn and looked out the window to see that it was getting dark. I got into my pjs and snuggled into the covers and fell asleep.

When I woke up I couldn't hear anything in the house. It was morning so I should have heard my parents making breakfast in the kitchen. I got up to find my parents or maybe a note they had left saying they were in town. There was no note. I found them in the living room, but something was horribly wrong. They were lying on the ground lifeless. Their bodies clawed, scratched, and shredded, except their faces which remained eerily untouched. Blood was everywhere and was still spilling from them. I was almost sick at the sight. I felt a twinge of guilt as if I had done this, but It couldn't have been though because I was asleep. Oh I wish I could have apologized to them about the fight. They were right about everything. I felt sadness plunge into my heart.

"I must remain strong," I thought, then I realized, I was now alone in this world. I knew no one, but the 2 lifeless bodies that were my parents. I cracked and shattered inside and sinking down to my knees, I started

to cry. The hot salty tears poured from my eyes and rolled down my face onto the ground mixing with my parents' blood.

My sadness was inescapable on my own so in my tear stricken state I did something with what little magic I had, not knowing what I did. Soon though I felt my sadness fade away. I looked around me and the sight no longer bothered me at all. I stood and felt nothing emotionally. Now out of my emotional hole, I began to think logically. I knew that someone would notice my parents' absence at work and would come looking. I didn't want to end up with someone I didn't know or in an orphanage, so I grabbed mom's special bag and threw all of my things, all of the food, utensils, clothing, books, and anything else of sentimental value or importance into the bag.

Then, with everything packed, I ran into the woods. I planned to live there for the rest of my life since they were already like a home for me. I used what little magic of mine was left and a spell book I had grabbed from home to form a cave on the side of a hill. It took a lot out of me, and I almost killed myself from the effort and passed out as soon as I had crawled inside.

It was 10 days until someone arrived at the house. I watched everything from the top of the trees. There were 2 men in a police car. They searched through the house and then wrote in a little book. I enhanced my vision with a spell and read what had been written.

"2 Deaths by wild animal"

"Child missing"

"Most likely snatched by the creature"

"Most likely dead"

It was good enough for me. When they left, I climbed down and went into the house, grabbed my parents bodies, and dragged them into the forest to bury them. That was the last time I saw those people.

Chapter 1

SELENE

5 Years Later

A year ago someone bought my old home. It was a family like mine, a wife and husband with a daughter a year or two older than me. I was surprised to find myself happy at the fact that someone now lived there. I had taken anything important to me out of the house and it had just stood there like a ghost.

Their daughter went into the forest by herself one day. Her parents weren't home and she walked in the shade of the trees. I watched her as she walked through the trees making sure no harm came to her as I knew there were many predators who would want her as a meal. So I traveled along the tree tops jumping from tree to tree as she walked below. For a little while I lost her because the leaves were too thick to see through. I went down to the lower branches and she was nowhere to be seen. Dropping down to the forest floor I proceeded to look for the girl. Suddenly I heard a scream coming from ahead of me. I ran towards the sound and found her. Her foot was caught in a tree root and her ankle was twisted badly.

"Please help me," she pleaded.

I would have to remove her most likely dislocated and possibly broken ankle to get her out. To distract her from the pain I decided to talk with her, while I examined her ankle more so.

"What is your name," I asked her softly?

"Alice," she replied painfully as I finished looking at her ankle.

"I need to remove your foot from the root. It will hurt a lot when I move it but it is necessary," I told her. I could see the fear in her eyes, but she was trying to be brave.

"I'll count to 3 and then I will remove you from the root okay? Ready...1...2...3," I said while yanking out her foot on three. She let out a blood curdling scream, but she was free.

"Thank you, but how will I get home?" she asked through tears of pain.

"I will help you," I promised her. I drew on the magic I had learned in my parents' books and levitated her off the ground a few inches. She started to look panicked.

"It is alright I am doing this to help you get home or to my home to heal you. Which would you prefer?" I asked her reassuringly.

"I don't think I can make it to my home. I'm in so much pain, it's almost unbearable," she replied whimpering. So I set off in the direction of my home.

When we reached my tree house I levitated both of us to the platform that was my front porch.

"Wow, your home is so beautiful," Alice said in amazement, now that she wasn't in as much pain since there was no weight on her ankle.

"Thank you, I made it myself a few years back after I got tired of living in a cave and became more skilled in my magic." I brought her to my table where I made potions and tinctures that I had learned and tried to make then recreate. It was also where I ate. I set her down atop the table and positioned her leg out in front of her. I tried to channel some healing magic but all I could do was ease her pain a little for that was all that I had learned. Then I grabbed a couple of vials off the shelf. I gave her one and kept the other.

"Drink the one I just gave you. It will relieve most of the pain for a little, I will fix your ankle once it takes effect," I told her. She looked at me suspiciously, but drank it anyway. After a minute she couldn't feel a thing in her ankle and I fixed her ankle just as I had with mine a year back. That had not been fun and I had no pain reliever potion, unlike Alice, and I had felt everything. Then I took my potion that I had grabbed, opened it and poured the fluid on my hands. I proceeded to rub it on her ankle. I saw her wince a little out of the corner of my eye. This made sense as the potion I had given her wasn't a strong one and only lasted a few minutes.

"The stuff I put on your ankle will bring down the swelling, but you will not be able to walk on that ankle for awhile, and I suggest you go to a doctor to look at it when we get you home," I told her. She nodded her head in understanding.

I levitated her back up off the table and back down to the forest floor. She started to make sounds of pain and I tried again to use some healing magic, but most of my magic was being used up to levitate her, it was not an easy thing.

Soon we came to her house where her parents had returned home and were frantically searching for their missing child. They saw us and came running outside. I set Alice down and she gasped in pain as her weight returned to her ankle. I let her lean on me for support. I didn't want her parents knowing I was magical, most people would freak out about it, plus magical law said I couldn't reveal magic. Unless it was necessary, like with Alice. Her parents saw us hobbling our way out of the woods and rushed out to her. They embraced her and looked her over making sure she was okay and started freaking out over her ankle. They turned to me thinking I had done this and started yelling at me and threatening me.

Alice hobbled in between her parents and I and yelled back at her parents,

"She didn't hurt me, I went off into the woods for a walk and my foot got caught in a root and I hurt my ankle. She appeared and saved me. Then she brought me back home. So stop treating her like a villain." Her parents stopped and looked strangely at me.

"Thank you," the mother finally said, " I am eternally grateful for your help. What is your name, child?" I thought for a minute. I didn't want to use my birth name as that name no longer applied to me, so I made one up.

"Selene Woods," I finally said, " I live in the woods with my parents. We try to stay away from society. Dad doesn't like it that much, but the woods are a great home to us." I lied to her of course. I couldn't let her know the truth about me. Alice gave me a look and then understood I was trying to hide my life.

"Well thank you again Selene, if there is anything we could do for you just let us know,: the mother said.

"Thank you, there is something I need, if anyone comes looking for my family and I, send them away or let us know please," I told her.

"I will do so," she replied as Alice's father carried Alice inside the house.

Chapter 2
ALICE
6 years later

A visitor showed up at our door on a hot day at the end of September. He knocked on our front door which we had recently repainted a stormy gray. My mom answered the door and almost jumped in surprise when she realized it wasn't someone she knew.

"What do you want?" she asked the stranger.

"I am looking for a girl. She was said to live here, do you know where this person is," he replied and showed my mom a picture. The way he spoke sent a shiver up my spine, but I was unsure as to why.

"I...I don't know who you mean," my mom stuttered looking at the photo. I caught a glimpse of it and saw Selene in full detail.

"Yes you do, you're giving it away in your expression and voice," the stranger spoke in a calm tone.

"Can you please wait out on the porch while we go and fetch her then?" my mom asked quickly.

"Of course," he said and went and sat on our porch swing. My mom closed the door with a bang and walked quickly over to me.

"Go to Selene and tell her there is a man who wishes to speak to her and won't leave until he sees her. You are the only one of us who knows where she lives in the forest." So I went out back and ran into the forest to Selene's tree house being very careful to avoid the tree roots.

SELENE

I was reading one of the spell books that I had acquired when I heard Alice down below on the forest floor calling my name. I walked out to my porch and there she was. *What is she doing here?* I had not seen Alice in a while. Last time was over 3 months ago when her parents wanted me to have dinner with them. I levitated myself down to the forest floor to meet her.

"What is it Alice?" I asked her," I have not seen you for awhile."

"There is a strange man at our door asking for you," She said quickly.

"Is he a possible threat to me?" I asked.

"I'm not sure, but he has a picture of you," Alice replied. *How did this man know of me and how did he have a picture of me?*

"Go and bring the man here Alice, then I can see for myself," I told her.

"Okay." Alice said unsure. She left the clearing and I wondered what this man wanted?

She returned a few minutes later with a man. She was definitely right. This person didn't look like a threat, but people can easily disguise themselves.

"Who are you stranger, and what do you want?" I asked the man.

"I am Robert Johnson and I am here to offer you an opportunity," he said, seeing that I was who he was looking for.

"Alice, you can go home, tell your mom that everything is well," I said. Alice looked at me questioningly and I looked back at her sternly and she left.

"What is this offer you speak of Robert?" I asked once Alice was out of earshot.

"The offer is for a scholarship at a school for the mystical arts, magic to be precise. I know it may seem a bit farfetched-." I cut him off.

"You insult me," I said to him.

"Excuse me?" he asked.

"I know of the mystical arts and what not," I said, "You are insulting me, by making me seem ignorant."

"I see. My apologies Ms. I assumed that since you hadn't been to one of our schools before that you would know nothing of what I speak, but since you do, let me restart. You have been offered a spot at Tripence Academy. It is a very prestigious institution. Not many get in," he said.

"Why do you want me?" I asked.

"You seem to have an affinity with magic according to our

records and we mages like to know where everyone's skills lie," Robert said.

"That is... understandable," I said suspiciously. Personally I think they just wanted to keep track of who was a threat or not.

"Why don't you come inside for a drink or snack?"

"Of course, I would love to meet your family," Robert said. So I levitated myself up to my porch and watched Robert levitate himself up after me. So he wasn't lying about being a mage. I quickly made some lemonade and a fruit salad.

"So where are your parents Selene?" Robert asked innocently.

"Out back," I answered.

"May I speak with them?"

"Later."

We ate and drank in silence for a while, and then he asked,

"Are you interested in coming to the Academy or not?"

"I think it is an interesting offer and it has been a long time since I've been away from home, but I'll need a little longer to make up my mind, if that's all right," I told him.

"Very well, may I meet you parents, please? Perhaps they can convince you to go," Robert said.

"Follow me," I told him. I walked through the house to the back patio and levitated myself down to the forest floor. I looked up and he was floating down behind me. We walked over to a small clearing where a stack of rocks stood and a small flower garden.

"I don't understand," Robert said, "Are your parents shape shifters and are the rocks and flowers?"

"No," I told him, "They are markers for where their graves are." I pointed to the rocks. "That is where father is."

Then I pointed to the flowers.

"That is where mother is."

"I'm so sorry I had no idea, when did they pass?" Robert apologized.

"About 11 years ago. I don't know what happened, I woke up and their bodies were torn apart in the living room. People came by and said it was a wild animal," I told him, "but I'm not so sure that is what happened."

"What do you mean?" he asked.

"I just feel that it's my fault for some reason, but I don't know why," I told him.

"It's natural to feel that way, but don't let it get to you. So about the Academy, will you go?" he asked.

I thought for a minute, but something in me answered before I could make up my mind.

"Yes," I said surprising myself.

"Great, here is the paperwork and once you fill it out they will disappear and be sent to the Academy," he said handing me a stack of papers, "then October 1st a blue glowing stone will appear in your home, be prepared with everything you need. Then grab hold of the stone and it will transport you to the school."

"Thank you," I told him.

"Now I must go, there are more people that I must tell that they got in, goodbye," he said and with that he disappeared, probably teleporting to the next person's house. I looked back at my parent's graves and saw that bright moss was now growing on the rocks and the flowers looked brighter and straighter. My parents were happy that I was going to this school.

I finished the paperwork that night and just as Robert said, it disappeared once I was done with it. I had two days to get ready till the 1st. I went to grab my mother's special bag. It looked like a regular old black messenger bag, but it was special because it was a never ending bag. It never filled up and it never got heavier no matter what you put in it. I started packing my clothes I had made over the years, my mom's old clothes and my dad's old clothes. I grabbed all of the magic books and normal books and threw them in too. I grabbed my potions and tinctures and put them in the bag as well. I grabbed all my herbs making sure they were stored properly. Then I threw in some blankets and food, just in case. Then I grabbed some items that were special to me, like my special rock and my plant.

Next morning I went to Alice's house. Her mom was home with Alice. When I got to their back porch Alice's mom ran out and hugged me. I was shocked and just stood straight. She composed herself and took a step back.

"I was worried about you," she said, "and I've never formally said this, but I think of you as another daughter of mine." I looked at her slightly shocked.

"Thank you, it's nice for someone to think of me like that," I told her and that was the truth. I hadn't had a mother in a long time. I had almost forgotten what it felt like.

"I came here to tell you that I'm going to be going away for awhile. That man gave me a scholarship to a boarding school that my grandparents had set up for me. They wanted me to have a proper education and not what my parents called education apparently. I'll be leaving tomorrow," I told her. She looked at me stunned, but eventually she said,

"Alright then, be careful while you are gone." I could tell she thought that it was a mistake. I went up to her and hugged her and she hugged back.

"Don't worry I'll be fine," I reassured her. I walked over towards Alice and whispered to her,

"Look after my home while I'm away." I stepped back and she nodded her head. We separated and I left. For the rest of the day I finished up packing and waited for the stone the next day.

The stone arrived in the morning around 7:30. It made a whistling sound that woke me up with a start. I saw the stone floating just outside my door. I dressed quickly in a plain black t-shirt and jeans, my father's cloak, and my boots which I had laid out the night before. Then I grabbed my bag and the staff that I had made in the spring. It was almost my height, and I had put a crystal at the top and charged it with magic. This way the staff could be used for fighting and wielding magic. I went up to the floating stone and grabbed it in my free hand. I brought my hand to my chest and closed my eyes. I felt a whooshing and knew I was no longer in my home.

Chapter 3

I opened my eyes to a courtyard with walls and a golden gate with the letters T and A formed from the metal bars. A parking lot was on my left and different sport courts and fields to my right... In front of me was a massive old looking building at least 3 stories if not more high. I looked around and saw students streaming into the building through what I guessed to be the main doors. The students looked to be a mixture of humans, humanoids and other mystical beings. I saw a group of satyrs walk by and a group of nymphs in the corner laughing. It was incredible. Suddenly I heard a woman's voice through all of the noise of the crowd.

"First years please come and stand by me for registration."

I saw a group of people with bags and luggage heading over towards the voice and I decided to follow them. As I reached the main doors the woman had a crowd around her. They all had bags and I assumed that they were first years just like me. I joined the group and waited for the woman to speak. When no one else joined the crowd the woman began.

"Welcome first years to Tripence Academy. Everyone here wishes you a successful first year in your learning. Now in just a little while all of you will follow me to registration where you will get your room number, your school ID and a few permission slips to be filled out. Look for the sign above the doors to find out which door you need to go in. It is alphabetical by last name. Then once you are done, you are free to go to your dorm room to unpack and meet your roommates. Then at 9am sharp go to the meeting hall for opening ceremonies. Now follow me to registration." She said walking into the building. After a second, everyone followed her. We walked into the building and it was a sight to behold.

There was a stained glass roof made up of a million different shards all glittering and sparkling in the morning sunlight making swirling shapes that represented different types of magic. The roof was arched and pillars, spaced out on the sides of the walls running the full length of the room, held up each end of the arch. In between each pillar there was a door or hallway where students went in and out. We followed the guide through the second door on the left. It led to a similar looking room except that there were signs with letters on them and it was far shorter than the other hallway.

"This is the registration hall, and for those of you who were wondering we were just in the main hall. Please line up in front of the door that contains the first letter of your last name," she said. I lined up in front of the door that said "U-Z". There were about 5 other people in line in front of me. One by one they went in and came out a few minutes later. Then it was finally my turn. I walked in through the door and saw a woman sitting at a desk with files in front of her. She had long gray hair and a petite figure.

"Have a seat please," she said and I sat down.

"Name," she said in a demanding yet bored tone. She probably did this for every person that walked in here.

"Selene Woods," I told her. She flipped through her files and then pulled one out.

"Oh yes, Mrs. Woods. I've never heard of that family name before, but there is a first time for everything. Let's see here, your dorm room is number 2305. Here is your student ID and a map of the school, as well as a bag of guide stones in case you ever get lost," she said and handed me a large sheet of paper, a cloth bag, and a thin piece of plastic with my name, year, and photo on it.

"When you walk out the door, turn right, walk through the wall and the elevator is on your second left. Type in your room number to get to your room," she said. I stood up and left. I turned right and went to the wall. I hesitated a little and then walked to it and passed right through. I found my elevator and typed in my room number. The elevator went up 2 floors and then to my surprise to the left and then forwards. The elevator doors opened to a dark oak door with the number 2305 burned into it. I stepped out of the elevator, whose doors closed once I was out. I walked up to the door, turned the handle and went inside.

The first thing I saw was what I believed to be the common room. There was a blue fire burning in the fireplace with long couches parallel to it and a TV above it. There was a kitchenette in the corner with a mini fridge, cabinetry, a small sink, and a few appliances. The walls were a light gray that complimented the dark oak flooring. There were two doors leading off from the main room. I walked up to one and the words Irene Murray were written on the door. I tried to turn the handle and a small shock went up my arm. I jumped back in surprise. I went to try the other door fully expecting another shock and found that I could turn the handle with no shock at all. I looked at the door and saw that my name was on it.

Oh, so the other door must lead to my roommate's room. No wonder it didn't open for me, it must have some kind of spell on it so only the student whose name was on the door could come in. I was amazed at the level of magic. I walked into my room and closed the door behind me. My room had dark blue walls and the floors matching that of the common room outside. There were five large bookshelves along one wall, a bed tucked into the corner and an oak desk in the middle of the room with a wheeled desk chair to sit on. There were two doors leading off from the main room. One of them led to a large walk in closet and the other to a spacious bathroom.

There was a bay window with 3 fluffy pillows in between the bed and bookshelves. I went and sat on the bed with its sheets and pillows matching the color of the walls. I opened my bag and said, "Books come out and place yourselves in alphabetical order by the author's last name."

All of my books flew out of my bag and did as I said. Then I told the clothes to go into the closet with my clothes in the middle, dads to the left, and moms to the right. I then told my other possessions to put themselves wherever they liked. I placed my staff in the corner of the room closest to me and laid down on top of the sheets. I looked at the clock on the wall, it was only a little after 8 o'clock so I had about an hour of nothing to do until the assembly. Then I heard a commotion outside my door and sat up.

I wonder who that is. I stood up, grabbed my staff and headed to the door.

Chapter 4
IRENE

This is the worst day ever. My parents made me late with all of their pictures and hugs and kisses saying they'd miss me and whatnot. While I was already running late because I couldn't find the top that I wanted that would have totally matched my white shorts, but instead I had to wear something else. I arrived while everyone was in registration and had to use my previous knowledge of the school to find my way. Then when I finally got there everyone was almost gone, so I had to hurriedly find my door, get my room number and get to the elevator.

"HUH." I sighed angrily. When I finally got to the damn room the door was already open, which means my roommate got here first and I like to be first. I dropped my bags on the common room floor.

"Could anything else go wrong," I mutter under my breath. My question was quickly answered when suddenly my roommate's door flew open and she was standing there in a black cloak holding a fighting staff.

Great, now I'm going to die.

"Sorry if I startled you. I'm not used to being around people," she said. She put down her staff just inside her door.

"Whatever," I told her. Jokingly, I added, "if you're really sorry you can help me with my bags." She came over and surprisingly grabbed two of my bags and headed towards my door.

"Um...thanks," I said. I opened the door so we could put my bags down. The room was a lilac purple, my favorite color, with nice dark flooring. The girl looked around in interest and then disgust.

"What's wrong now?" I asked.

"My room is a different color," she said interestingly, "good thing too because this room is way too bright and girly," she then said disgusted.

"Get out and go back to your own room then," I shouted at her.

"Great I got a goth girl for a roommate," I thought. She left my room and went into her own.

Good now maybe I'll have some peace and quiet while I unpacked. I opened my bags and took out my clothes and placed them into the closet. Then I place all of my trinkets on the shelves and the desk. Then I placed my favorite blanket and pillow on the bed then decided to lie down.

The assembly isn't until 9. I looked at the clock and saw that it was 8:30 already. "Damn I really wanted to take a nap," I muttered. I hadn't slept much last night in preparation for today. Instead of sleeping I went to the closet and found my pink crop top that I had been looking for earlier and put it on. Then I went to the bathroom and quickly checked my blonde hair to make sure that there weren't any brown roots showing, and reapplied my makeup to my beautiful blue eyes and perfectly tanned skin. When I was satisfied with my looks I went out into the common room where my pesky roommate was sitting on one of the couches looking at the fire.

SELENE

Irene came out of her room less angry then she had entered it. I decided against talking to her and just continued to stare at the fire, so I wouldn't anger her more. I always liked how fire moved, with its sparks and pops, the twisting and twirling of the flames. The sound that it makes brings me back to the comforts of home, on a snowy night watching the flames and listening to the crackle of the fire.

"Come on," Irene said, breaking me out of my trance, " the assembly is about to start and I've been late enough for one day."

"Alright then you go on ahead I have to grab something from my room," I told her. I stood up and went to my room and found my mother's pendant. It was a glass bulb with smoke swirling inside of it. It had the carving of a black dragon claw holding the bulb. My mom used to wear it for very special occasions and I thought it was fitting to wear it now. I removed my cloak and put it in the closet, then walked out of the room. To my surprise Irene was still there.

"Come along with you," she said. She reached into a cloth bag and pulled out a small stone. She whispered something to it and it lit up in a brilliant blue light and it started floating to the door.

"Come on, before it floats away," she told me. I followed; realizing that the stone was a guide stone and it was taking us most likely to the assembly since it was almost 9. We followed it down twisting corridors into a large room. It looked similar to the main hall in architecture with columns, but no glass roof. There was, on the opposite end of the room, a stage with rows and rows of chairs in front of it . Every first year that was in the welcome group and more were there.

Chapter 5

Most seats were already filled up, but I found one in the back. I sat down and waited for whatever was supposed to happen while staring at the stage with the podium topping it. It only took a few minutes before a woman in a blue pantsuit walked on stage to the podium.

"Good morning first years, to Tripence Academy, I am Dean Autumn. Now in just a few minutes you are going to start the journey on your magical education and becoming great mages. Now here are a few basic things you'll need to know before going into this and yes, I know that some of you already know this, but it can't hurt to review it."

"Now, there are 3 groups of magic classification, the physical, the spiritual, and the mental. People can be one or more of these classifications. Now physical magic includes the main 4 elements: water, fire, earth, and air. Everyone should know these. Everyone is at least strong in one element and when you meet with your counselor they will discover your strengths and weaknesses with these elements. Now there are two other main branches that come off of the main 4. There is physical and magical defense. In this class you will learn how to defend yourself using magic and how to use magic to attack. As well as how to use weapons such as swords, staffs, knives etc. Any use of attack magic on school grounds, not permitted by a teacher, will have consequences. The other branch of magic is healing. This is optional for any students and focuses on tincture, potions, and spells to help heal, or relieve pain and injuries, there are also other branches of potion making off of this, but I'm not going to get into that today."

"Now the next of the three is mental magic. This branch is quite rare, only one maybe two of you will be mentalists if that. Mental magic is where a mage is able to do many types of magic using only thought. Once again using this in any form of attack will have consequences. Finally the last of the main 3 is spiritual magic. This is a dangerous magic and not common but not as rare as mental magic. If you have spiritual magic you must learn how to control it. It focuses on the spirit, how to look, control, and touch them for some examples."

"Now with that out of the way we can get on to classes. You will meet with your council member, who will test you for your elements and assign you your classes. When I call your name please stand." She started listing off names. With every name called the person would stand up and disappear. It freaked me out at first, but then after a few names it got less freaky.

"Selene Woods," Dean Autumn said. Shakily I stood and my vision blurred for a second and then it was over. I found myself in a dimly lit room with a man staring intensely at me.

"Who are you?" I asked the stranger sitting across from me.

"I am counselor Pyro, please have a seat," the man said, gesturing to the chair across the desk. I took a seat in the chair.

"So, you are Selene Woods. I must admit I have never heard of the Woods family before," he said questioningly.

"That's because it is not my birth name. It's a name I took when I was 10," I told him.

"Oh, and what is your birth name?" he asked.

"I rather not say, the name brings painful memories. Besides, I am no longer the person I once was so it does not matter," I said.

"I see, well anyway let's get to know you a bit more. Any magical experience?" he asked.

"A little from what I read in my parents' books, but I'm not the world's greatest teacher," I told him. He jotted a note onto a paper.

"Very well then let's get onto the testing," he said. Council member Pyro reached behind his desk and pulled out a tray. On it was a candle, a glass of water, and a pot of soil.

"This is the element test," he said, "I will test you on each element separately."

"What about air?" I asked him.

"Air is all around us, as soon as you came in I knew your affinity for air, which might I say, is above average," he told me, "Now place your hand into the soil in the pot." I did as I was told and as soon as I did a bright green sprout poked out from the earth and grew into a fully bloomed white lilac. He jotted down another note.

"Looks like you have a high affinity for earth," Pyro said.

That made sense always felt connected to the forest I lived in. Thinking about it made me feel a bit homesick.

"Now touch the water," he said. I touched the glass and a few small ripples appeared in the glass. He jotted down another note.

"You have an average affinity with water, we will work on growing it throughout the school year," Pyro told me, "Now squeeze the candle wick between your fingers and picture fire, then when you are ready snap those two fingers." I followed his instructions and when I was ready I snapped my thumb and middle fingers across the wick. A small blue flame appeared when I did. It was so beautiful; I couldn't help but stare at it. It swayed slightly back and forth. Pyro said something to me, but I didn't hear him. I was mesmerized by this small flame. I found myself reaching out to it. The closer I got, the more it grew, and the more I was attracted to it. I wanted to be with the fire. It wanted me to be with it. Pyro was writing something down at his desk and still talking, but I just kept staring. I reached my hand into the flame and it shot up into a huge fireball. Pyro looked up from the new light and quickly removed my hand from the fire, putting the fire out.

My hand wasn't burnt at all, it wasn't even warm. I shook my head clearing the left over effects.

"WHAT DID YOU DO?!" Pyro asked/yelled at me.

"I don't know, I was just looking at the fire and I wanted to touch it, you tell me what just happened!" I yelled back at him slightly frightened by how he was reacting.

"What you just did was show that you have more of an affinity with fire than I thought," he told me, still with a tone of anger in his voice and scribbled out something on the paper and jotted down another note, "Alright, let's just move on. Do you want to learn healing?"

"Um...sure," I said after a second.

"Alright then give me a minute and I will have your schedule ready," he said.

"What about testing for spiritual and mental magic?" I asked.

He stopped what he was doing and looked at me.

"The mental test has killed people who weren't mentalists and the spiritual test has almost killed or severely crippled students who weren't spiritual mages, so unless you show signs that you are one of them or have family background in those magic, we won't test for it," he said seriously.

"Ok," I told him.

"Maybe you should find a test that doesn't kill people," I thought.

"Here is your schedule, classes start tomorrow. You'll have healing class in the second half of the year and have potion making this half. The rest of the day is yours to do whatever you want. Lunch is at noon, dinner at 8pm, and breakfast is always at 8am. Have a good day Mrs. Woods," Pyro said coldly.

"Good day Councilor Pyro," I said just as coldly as my vision started to blur again and I found myself outside of my dorm room.

COUNCIL MEMBER PYRO

After Selene left, I quickly got up from my desk and made my way to the Dean's office. I knocked on her door and got her answer to come in.

"Good morning Dean Autumn," I said.

"Good morning Pyro, what can I do for you?" she asked.

"Who is Selene Woods?" I asked quickly.

"A student, your student if I remember correctly, you should have met her already," Autumn said confused.

"Yes, I did, but when I asked her about her family name she told me it wasn't Woods that she had a different name. Then when I asked her what it was, she refused to tell me," I told her.

"Hmm...this is troubling, we will have to keep an eye on her," Autumn said.

"Yes, but do you know who she really is?" I asked impatiently.

"I have no clue, I will speak to her recruiter and see if they know. Why do you ask?"

"Selene did something strange with the fire test,"

"What did she do?" Autumn asked curiously.

"I'm not sure. I looked away to write in my notes then I looked up and the blue fire from her candle was surrounding her hand and arm. I stopped her and the fire went out. It almost looked like she was in a trance, just staring at the fire on her hand. The strangest part was that her hand wasn't burnt after."

"Thank you for letting me know. I'll look into this. Please go back to your office Pyro and I'll call you back once I've spoken to her recruiter," she said. I left and returned to my office. She called me up to her office not even a half hour later.

Chapter 6
SELENE

I opened the door to the dorm and saw Irene asleep on one of the couches. I decided against disturbing her and went to my room. I had an hour till lunch and nothing to do, so I decided to try and find the dining hall. I took out the paper that they had given me at registration. I opened it and all of a sudden a miniature 3D version of the school was in my hands.

"Which room would you like to find?" a voice called.

"Who's there?" I asked.

"I am Map, what would you like to find today?" Map asked.

Ok, this is a little freaky.

"The dining hall please," I told the map.

"Finding destination, calculating route," Map said. Then the mini school zoomed in on my room. It started to zoom out a little and I could see in between the different floors. Then a lighted strip of light appeared connecting my room to what I guessed was the Dining Hall. It wasn't all that far from here.

"Route calculated, Dining Hall, room 105," Map said. So I went to go and look for it to be early for lunch. I came out of my room and heard Irene on the phone with someone in her room. I walked out of the dorm and went to the elevator. The Dining Hall's room number was 105, so I tried that in the elevator since it was how I got to my dorm room. The elevator went up to my surprise and to the right and backwards. On the map the Dining Hall was on the first floor. The doors opened to an ornate door with carvings of different magical symbols. Then I saw a name on the door, Dean Autumn. I had found the Dean's office. I crept up to the door and heard an angry voice that I recognized, I was Pyro.

"What is he doing here?" I muttered and got closer to the door.

"Who is she, Autumn?" I heard Pyro ask.

"Our student records say that she is Selene Woods, there is no other name, her recruiter was busy but said he'll come in as soon as he can, this is all I can tell you Pyro," Dean Autumn said. They were talking about me. It was because I told Pyro that Selene

Woods wasn't my birth name. That guy had reported me. I heard Pyro start to leave and I hurried back to the elevator and went back to my room.

I walked in not even noticing Irene sitting on the couch and went straight to my room. So many thoughts swirled in my head. Do they know my birth name? Was Pyro just curious or was he genuinely concerned? Does this have nothing to do with my name and it's just because of the weird thing that happened with the fire? I found myself getting very confused and my head started to hurt. I sat down on the floor and started meditating, trying to control my thoughts. Slowly my headache decreased and then it was gone. I took out my schedule and read over what my classes were tomorrow. I was half way through when I heard a knock on the door. I went and opened it and Irene was standing there in the doorway.

"Listen," she said quietly, "this morning I was in a bad mood and I know I may have offended you or hurt your feelings, but I don't want us to have bad blood. So I am here to apologize for my earlier behavior."

"I accept your apology, but I wasn't hurt by what you said," I told her.

"Then why have you been giving me the silent treatment?" she asked, upset.

"I thought it would be best if you cooled off on your own. Most of the time talking to people when they are in a bad mood just makes them angrier," I told her. This was at least true for my pet rabbit. I forgot to feed her once and then she went off in a huff and came back the next day all lovey.

"That is actually pretty smart. I just realized I never got your name," she said.

"Selene Woods," I told her.

"Great to meet you Selene, can we start over and be friends?" She asked.

"Of course," I told her.

"Great, now come on it's almost lunch," She said and playfully pulled me out of my room.

It didn't take long for her to find the Dining Hall.

"How do you know where you are going in this place?" I asked her.

"My dad is a professor here and I used to go to work with him, this place is pretty much my second home," She said.

"Wow, I've never been here before. Until earlier this week, I didn't even know this place existed," I said.

"Really, how did you get in then?" She asked, shocked.

"A man came to my house and told me that there was a place for me at this school and I decided to take it," I told her.

"Cool, you must have been really lucky to get in. What did your parents think?" She asked. I froze. At this point we had reached the cafeteria doors and were going inside.

"Can we talk more about this back in the dorm room?" I asked hoping she wouldn't push for more details.

"Okay, if that's what you want. I'm going to go eat lunch with my friends, you're welcome to join us if you like," she said politely looking in the direction of her friends. I saw them and they weren't my kind of people. They were pretty and popular, all giggling over things on their phones.

"No thanks, I'm going to sit in the corner over there," I said, pointing to the opposite corner her friends were sitting at.

"Okay, go have a good lunch," Irene said and ran off to meet with her friends. I made my way to the line to get some food and saw just empty plates that people were picking up and bringing to their table. Then I realized that as they got to their table, food appeared on the empty plate.

Cool. I grabbed my plate and made for an empty table. When I sat down my plate changed. It now had a fruit salad and my favorite venison soup that I would make back home. While I was eating a girl came over and sat across from me. She was short and skinny with long braided blond hair, hazel eyes and was a pasty pale.

"Hi, I'm Sarah. This is my first day here and I don't know that many people and I thought since you're here sitting by yourself I could sit with you. You looked lonely," she said perkily

"I'm Selene, this is my first day too and the only person I know is over there," I said pointing to Irene's table, "They aren't my type of people."

"Mine neither, they're always so snobby unless they want something from you, then they act all nice and fake. I'm sorry you have to have one as your roommate. One of them used to be my friend and just abused my friendship. They tried to get me to drink alcohol and hook up with a guy I didn't even know just because he was hot and popular. I'm so glad I got out of that," Sarah said. Then a guy came and sat next to Sarah. He was tall and had short brown hair, tan, and bright blue eyes.

"So is this our table now?" he asked her.

"Maybe, you'll have to ask the person who got here first," Sarah answered him.

"Hey, I'm Jake, Sarah's oldest friend. We've known each other since we were pretty much born," he said.

"Hi, I'm Selene," I told him.

"So is this our table now?" he asked with a slight smile.

"I guess," I told him.

"Great."

"Is there anyone else that will be sitting here?" I asked looking at Sarah. Before she could answer another guy showed up. He was tall, dark colored, chocolate brown eyes and hair.

"Jake, what up my dude," He said and then noticed me.

"Who's she?" he asked.

"This is Selene, our new lunch pal," Sarah chimed in.

"I can speak, you know," I said. I was starting to get annoyed with people coming over here that I don't know.

"Feisty, I like it. I'm Noah," he said and offered his hand as he sat down on Sarah's other side. I took it and he gave me a firm shake.

"A.K.A. my boyfriend," Sarah said.

"Oh, good for you," I said. I went on eating my food while they talked about things I didn't care for. Sarah and Noah were making goo goo eyes at each other and acting how I thought most couples acted together. I felt bad for Jake. He must have had to sit through a lot of these.

"So, what about you Selene?" Jake asked, coming and sitting next to me, prying away from Sarah and Noah.

"What about me?" I asked him.

29

"Well for starters, where do you live?" he asked.

"In a tree house," I answered him.

"Cool, your parents bought you a tree house to live in, that is really awesome," he said.

"Um... not quite," I told him.

"What do you mean, did you run away from home or something?" he asked.

"No, um, I don't want to say here if that's ok with you," I told him. Then a bell rang signifying the end of lunch. I stood up as all of the plates floated away into one of the side rooms, most likely the kitchen.

"Well, how about we meet up later in the school garden, say around 5?" he asked, pleading with his eyes.

"Why would you want to do that, you only just met me?" I asked him and started walking to the door.

"I think you're interesting and really pretty and I want to be better friends with you since we will probably be sitting with each other at meals for the rest of the year and now I'm babbling like an idiot," he said walking quickly to catch up with me.

"Well thank you for the compliments and I don't think you're an idiot. Alright, I guess it couldn't hurt, I'll see you at 5," I said. He excitedly walked up to my side and walked me to the elevator. He told me he was looking forward to seeing me tonight and then the doors closed. As the elevator went up I had to wonder if he wanted something more from me then my friendship.

Chapter 7

When 4:30 came around the sun had started to set. The sky was ablaze in the dying light of the sun. I opened my window to get some of the cool autumn air in the stuffy dorm room. I was getting ready for my meeting with Jake when a knock on the door stopped me. I opened it and saw Irene standing at the threshold.

"I was wondering, what were you going to tell me, before we got to the cafeteria?" She asked politely. I had almost forgotten that she asked about my parents.

"Um...come on in and I'll tell you," I said nervously. She came in and sat at my desk and I closed the door. I walked over to the window seat and sat. The sun's rays turned my white hair a golden color.

"So what do, your parents do?" she asked.

"Nothing," I told her.

"What, why?" she asked laughing.

"Because they died when I was six," I told her. She immediately stopped laughing.

"I'm so sorry. What happened?" she asked.

"I don't know, I just found them dead one morning," I told her calmly.

"That must have been awful. What happened afterwards?" she asked.

"It wasn't too bad; I went into the woods behind my house. They were always more of a home to me than my actual home was. Besides now I live in a tree house in those woods," I told her, missing home more than ever. My head started hurting again.

"You know, you didn't have to tell me this, most people wouldn't tell anyone about something like that, but you did. So thank you for trusting me," she said.

"Of course, I don't want to hide things from my friends," I told her and got my thoughts and feeling under better control. The pain in my head began to fade...

"Alright, I'll make sure not to hide anything from you then," she said. Then she took a deep breath and quietly said,

"My mom isn't a mage." I looked at her slightly shocked. I was not expecting that.

"Please don't tell anyone. It's against the council's rules to have non-mages in mage families but my dad was friends with her before he went to school here and fell in love with her when he came back home. It is a really romantic story, but she doesn't know anything about magic. She thinks I'm at the boarding school my dad works at," She said.

"I won't tell anyone as long as you don't tell anyone about my thing," I said.

"Deal," She said, shaking my hand to seal the deal.

"Now if you'll excuse me I have a meeting with a friend to go to at 5 o'clock and it's almost 4:50, and I still have to get there," I said.

"Oh, yeah, of course, have fun," She said and left. I grabbed my cloak and put it on and as a last thought grabbed my mom's bag and put my staff in it just in case. Then I left with the map in hand and went to find the garden.

Jake was sitting on a bench at the front gate to the garden.

"I was hoping you would show up," he said.

"I said I would come, didn't I," I told him.

"Yeah well I've been stood up before," he said. I wondered what he meant by that. We walked into the gardens and found a fountain. I sat on the lip of the fountain and Jake sat next to me. The pitter patter of the water in the fountain was soothing for me.

"I like your cloak," he said.

"Thanks, it was my father's," I told him.

"Oh, cool, does your father not need it anymore?" he asked. I started getting a bit sad and my head hurt again.

"Not where he is," I told him, sighing.

"What do you mean," he asked?

"Both my mom and dad died when I was six," I told him sadly as the pain in my head increased.

"I'm so sorry I had no idea. Is that why you didn't want to tell me in the cafeteria?" he asked.

"Yes," I answered. We sat in silence for a little. My head was hurting more by the second. I couldn't control my memories and emotions. They all came flooding back to me. I was losing control.

"Why did you want to meet me, and tell me the truth this time?" I asked him, snapping myself away from my thoughts. A lightning bolt of pain shot through my head. He looked at me slightly shocked and then relaxed a little.

"Sarah told me to talk with you," he said.

"Why?" I asked.

"Well Sarah is a spiritual mage; she can see other people's souls. She told me that when she looked at you, she saw your soul," he said.

"What did it look like?" I asked, curious yet slightly fearful.

"It was bright, but had shadows twisting around inside. The main thing she saw was that your soul was cracked and broken in places. Then she saw spiritual chains wrapped all over all of the cracks trying to keep them from breaking and letting the shadows out. From what you just told me I'm not surprised that you're broken inside," he said.

"Yeah, I woke up in the morning and saw them in the living room," I said trying to hold in my emotions. My head kept on pounding, the beat matching to my increasing heart rate. He put his hand on my shoulder.

"It's okay to cry," he said and made me look into his big blue eyes. Suddenly the pain stopped and I looked back at him, not wanting these emotions. I had not felt like this in years. Something in his eyes made me think that it was okay to feel these emotions. I felt myself relinquish control on my emotions.

"Why don't you let yourself feel these things, it's natural to feel. You don't have to hold it in for me," he said. I felt the tears on my face before I felt the sadness. With each tear the pain in my head slowly increased. He watched me cry and through my tears, I told him,

"I don't like to feel emotion. It hurts me and it can hurt others."

"How would it hurt others," he asked?

"The night before my parents died, I was angry at them and I wish I could have apologized to them for being mad, but now it is too late, and I miss them so much," I said hugging myself. I started crying harder, letting all of the tears that had piled up over the years fall. They were hot and each one came with an old memory of me and my parents. My headache grew stronger with each memory. I started to bottle my emotions back up along with the memories. I couldn't take feeling these emotions again. It felt unnatural.

When I eventually gained control over them my head hurt a lot. Jake took one look at me and put his arms around me. I fell into his grasp letting the warmth from his arms and chest comfort me. The pain in my head ceased. He put his head on mine.

"I'm glad that I met you Selene. You're a great friend in trusting me," he said.

"I'm glad I have friends. I've never had that before. I've always been alone in this world. No family, no friends, no one I could trust," I told him, then thought of Alice, "Well maybe one person, my neighbor Alice. She's a nice girl." He looked down at me and removed me from his grasp.

"What is Alice like?" he asked.

"She is a curious girl, a year or two older than me. She would sometimes invite me for dinner and we would hang out at my place a lot," I told him. He looked at me processing what I had just said. Then I heard a branch snap behind us in the garden. I didn't realize that it had gotten so quiet. I looked behind me and saw no one.

"We should go," I told Jake.

"Ok," he said. We got up and went back inside the school, but I couldn't shake off the feeling that we were being watched.

Chapter 8

I woke up to the school's bell. It was the alarm saying that I had thirty minutes before breakfast. I went and took a shower, then dressed in a black turtleneck, leggings and black combat boots. I grabbed my bag and my schedule, and then hurried to breakfast.

Irene was already there sitting with her friends. I grabbed a plate—it became sunny side eggs, wheat toast, and a fruit salad after I found Jake, Sarah, and Noah at the same table that we sat at for lunch and dinner yesterday.

"So what are your classes?" Sarah asked.

"Intro to air, physical combat, intro to fire, intro to water, potion making, earth 101, and then spell casting," I told her.

"Oh goody, I have intro to air and potion making with you," Sarah said.

"I have class with you for physical combat," Noah said and went back to eating.

"I have intro to air, intro to water, earth 101, and intro to fire with you Selene," Jake said.

"Great," I told them, I was happy that I would have my friends in some of my classes. After breakfast was over I walked with Sarah and Jake to Intro to air.

The classroom had about thirty desks, most filled with students by the time we arrived. There was a chalkboard at the front and a podium for the teacher. It's what I imagined a normal classroom to look like. We found three seats together in the middle and sat. The bell rang as the teacher walked in and began class.

"Good morning students and welcome to intro to air. Here you will learn the basics of air and how to control it. I am Mr. Nelson. Now are there any questions?" he asked. The hand of a young cyclops girl in the front row shot up and the teacher called on her.

"Will we learn how to levitate in this class?" she asked.

"Not in this class no, but next year you will," he said. She looked sad. I then saw that she had crutches next to her desk.

That's why she wants to learn how to levitate. I thought about teaching her how to levitate since I already knew how, but decided against it.

There must be a reason they do it this way.

"Any other questions?" he asked and no one raised their hand. He continued, "Good, now let's do something fun. We are going to learn how to make a ball of air in our hands. It's easy, if you just concentrate," he said. Then he demonstrated and a baseball sized swirling ball of air could be seen in his hands. I copied him and had a grapefruit sized ball of air passing from hand to hand on my first try. Some people struggled like Sarah. It took ten minutes for her and it was only a pea sized ball. Jake like me had gotten it on the first try, but his was a basketball sized and as he got bored he made a hoop out of air and started shooting his ball into the hoop.

"I have an above average affinity with air," he whispered to me. I joined him in the game and a few other students noticed and joined us. Soon we were all playing the game HORSE. When the bell rang an hour later everyone had some sized ball of air floating around the room.

"Good job class. Your homework is to practice making a larger ball of air and quicker. You will be timed next class," Mr. Nelson said.

My next class was physical combat. I was a little nervous but I found the place and opened the door. It was a large room with high ceilings. There were stands circling the outside of the room. Everyone was in the center of the room around a buff man and a woman with red hair. I walked up next to everyone.

"Hello, I'm Coach Swift and this is my co-teacher Coach Blood. Today you will learn how to defend and attack using a staff," the male coach said once everyone was around them. I got excited for today's class.

"We know some of you have fighting staffs of your own, given to you by family or friends or you just bought one, but for those of you who don't have one, a staff will be provided by the school. If it breaks then you will have to pay for it. Now at the end of the week we will have a tournament to see who is the best with their staff," Coach Swift continued.

"Does anyone have questions?" Coach Blood asked. No one raised their hands.

"Good. Then those of you who don't have a staff come with me and those of you that do go to Coach Swift," she said. I walked over to Coach Swift seeing other students with staffs in their hands heading the same direction. I pulled my staff out from my bag and made it over to the Coach. He did a close look at each of our staffs in turn making sure there weren't any enhancements that would lead to cheating. I was glad to see that my staff was not the only one with a gemstone on the top. Coach Swift looked over mine and said it was cleared, so I went to stand in the middle of the room again.

After ten minutes everyone had a staff. The coaches showed us some basic moves and we practiced them against fighting dummies. I already knew most of the moves from when I had trained myself from books. Noah was a few dummies down from me and he was doing quite well to my surprise. I was slightly impressed. Most of the students on the other hand, were either getting the hang of the movements or were still struggling. Soon class was over and I walked out feeling ready for Friday.

My next class was intro to fire and I met Jake at the door. We walked in and I saw a large fire pit with a big blazing fire at the center of it. There were metal benches in a circle around the fire. Jake and I sat down in the second row.

"Good morning students, welcome to Intro to fire. I am Mr. Davis. First before we start, I have some ground rules to go over. There is no throwing fire without permission from me. If someone does it is a detention or suspension. Fire is a dangerous element, so let's all be very careful because you will get burnt," he said,

"To start class today I want to go over the fundamentals of fire. Fire has strong emotional ties to the user, so we recommend trying to remove your emotions when using fire or try being in control of your emotions, especially anger or sadness as they cause more. Fire can be created out of nothing, but only the most skilled mages are able to. It takes them years to learn how to do it though and they need a fuel source around to have any chance of creation from nothing, so please don't try. For students we work on calling the fire to us, which is how most mages use fire nowadays. Our first exercise is to call the fire to us and make a ball of fire." he said and demonstrated how to make a ball.

"Now you try," he said. I stared at the fire and tried to call the fire to me, but it didn't work for me. I tried to stay away from learning fire back home in case I accidentally burned down the forest so this was all new to me. I began feeling frustrated and tried to subdue the emotion, but it just grew with something in me adding to the frustration. I found myself staring more intensely at it and my emotions started to uncoil and exposed themselves to the flames. I wanted to touch the flames so badly, but I knew I would get burnt if I did.

My hand ended up betraying my mind and I reached towards the flames. Mr. Davis was distracted with another student and didn't notice me. I got closer to the flames. I was almost touching them when I suddenly felt a tug on my shoulders pulling me back, but I resisted the pull and went closer to the flames. I heard a call to the teacher from someone behind me and felt the tug again. This time it was too strong for me to resist and I fell back onto the floor. I was lying on the dirt floor still seeing the flames in my mind's eye looking up at the ceiling. The flames were so beautiful while they danced. I heard a muffled sound of someone talking, but I just kept staring at the ceiling, seeing the fire. I didn't want to move from the flames, they were so warm and comforting.

I was picked up into someone's arms and they started running away from the fire and out the classroom door. I looked towards the fire and started to reach towards the flames as we left the classroom, but my hand was grabbed and forced back to my side. I closed my eyes and saw the flames still flickering, but they got dimmer and dimmer the farther we got. My anger, frustration, sadness, and something else inside me got barred and caged back up once again. I felt satisfied with this and drifted into unconsciousness.

Chapter 9

I woke up on a soft bed with Jake staring over at me. He was sitting in a chair just staring at me. He saw my open eyes and visibly sighed. A nurse came over and helped me sit up.

"What happened?" I asked Jake, already afraid of the answer.

"You stuck your hands into the fire pit, I tried to pull you back, but you resisted me. It took two other students and Mr. Davis to finally pull you back. Then it looked like you were in some kind of trance. Mr. Davis said we had to get you to the infirmary and there was no way you were standing, so I picked you up and carried you here," Jake replied looking worried.

"How long was I out?" I asked.

"Not long, a minute or two maybe," he said, "What happened Selene?"

"I don't know. I did as Mr. Davis said. The next thing I know my body betrayed my mind and I wanted to go jump into the fire. That's all I remember before blacking out." I told him, sighing. I stood up, I was getting tired of laying on that bed.

"Are you sure you should be getting up?" Jake asked. Concern was etched on his face as he watched me stand.

"I'm fine now, you don't need to worry about me," I said grabbing my bag kind of harshly.

"This is why I don't let myself feel emotions. Something bad always happens," I said to him quietly. He looked at me silently.

We headed out of the infirmary and went back to class. Mr. Davis saw me and just stared.

"How did you do that," he asked?

"Do what," I asked him?

"It looked like you were becoming the fire, your hand was in the fire and yet you didn't get burnt. Any other person would have been burnt to a crisp," he said.

"I don't know, the fire was calling me, it wanted me to join it," I told him.

"It called to you. You didn't call it?" he asked.

"Yes," I said.

"I'll have to report this, but for now just relax and stay away from the fire. Wow, never thought I'd say that in this class," He said walking away. I sat on the very back bench and Jake sat next to me.

"I didn't want to say this in front of Mr. Davis but before you passed out it looked like the fire was in your eyes," Jake said. I looked at him and knew he wanted an answer for this.

"The eyes are the windows to the soul, they say. When I was in that trance my fire inside was coming out. All my sadness and anger that had been piled up over the years was released inside me, connecting me with the fire. It wanted the fire to ignite me and set it free," I told him. He looked at me slightly stunned.

"Promise me you won't do it again?" he asked, almost pleading with me.

"I promise," I said, knowing that I would break my promise. This wasn't something I could control, but if it made him feel better I would try.

I watched him go back to the fire and participate with the rest of the class. I turned my back to the fire, ignoring its call. I still had a half an hour of class still, so just for the sake of boredom, I found the fire inside of me that had almost been let out and reluctantly let a little of it out. I got angry all of a sudden and a memory from my past flared into my mind. It was the argument that I had with my parents the night before they died. I channeled that anger and the memory to my hand and out. And nothing happened.

Why would I think that would do anything? Suddenly a small flame sprouted in my open hand. I jumped up and it went out. I looked around, but no one had seen me. I decided to not tell anyone about this until I knew what it meant. I had a feeling it would get me into more trouble. I spent the rest of class staring away from the fire and reading one of my non magic books that I carried with me.

Lunch was next and I walked with Jake there. We sat at the regular table and soon Sarah and Noah soon joined us. Turned out both of them had intro to earth before lunch. We talked about our classes and how ridiculous it was that it was all the same homework for almost every class. Then Jake looked at me looking for approval and I gave it to him knowing what he was going to say.

"Something strange happened to Selene in fire class," he said.

"Like what, she is terrible at it," Noah said jokingly and laughed.

"No," I told him, "I was looking at the fire trying to call it to me to make a ball. Instead the fire called me to it and I almost jumped into the fire. If Jake wasn't there I probably would have." They looked at me with disbelief.

"That's really strange. I've never heard of that before and my dad is a fire teacher here," Sarah said.

I just ignored the rest of the conversation and went back to eating my lunch.

I left the Dining Hall and went to intro to water class with Jake.

"Are you alright," Jake asked?

"I'm not sure," I told him. I felt like I was falling into a hole and could never get out.

"I'll be fine," I assured him, but my words did nothing to assure me.

The water classroom looked just like the fire class room, but instead of a fire pit there was a pool of water.

"Good morning class, I am Mrs. Abernathy. I am super excited to teach you this year. I'm going to skip all of the stuff you have probably heard already today and tell you the one rule of water magic. There is a branch of water magic called blood magic which is forbidden. Anyone caught using this magic will have to go in front of The Council of Mages to face judgment. Ok? Ok. Now let's get on to fun stuff. As in most of your classes we are going to learn how to form a ball of water, but first I want to go over my classroom rules," she said.

"What is blood magic?" I whispered to Jake as Mrs. Abernathy droned on about meaningless things about classroom etiquette.

"It's like she said. It's a forbidden branch of magic, but basically, when learned, it can control the blood in a person's veins and can basically control a person," Jake whispered back, "There was a guy a few years ago that learned blood magic and was set on killing the whole council—all because he was mad at them for something they did.

"What's his name and who was he mad at?" I asked Jake.

"His name was John Adams and no one but he and the people he hunted knew why he did what he did. He killed ten mages and their families before he was caught and had his magic bound so he couldn't use it. Then they imprisoned him," he said.

Mrs. Abernathy started showing us how to form a ball of water and we stopped talking.

Jake and I got it on our third try and started passing them back and forth to each other just to entertain ourselves. By the end of class, we were both a little wet from popped balls of water we hadn't been able to catch. I dried Jake and myself off using some magic just before the bell rang. Like air, my homework was to practice making a ball of water.

I walked down to potion making with Sarah after saying goodbye to Jake. The teacher, Mrs. Angel, had us make a few basic healing potions like the ones I made back home. We gave them to the nurse once class was over. I went to my next class, earth 101 and sat outside on the main lawn next to Jake. It was a chilly fall day, so I pulled my sweater out of my bag and put it on.

We sat on the ground around the teacher, Mrs. Blackwood. She had us meditate and feel the earth beneath us. I listened to the trees sway and felt the grass underneath me. She then told us to try and bring a cloud of dirt up in front of us and compact it into a stone. I did as she said and felt each individual grain of dirt come to me. I thought of the dirt turning to stone and saw in my mind the dirt pressing together more and more. I felt a small rock form, about the size of my palm, and then it fell into my hand. Mrs. Blackwood had us shape something out of it, whatever we wanted. I thought of my parents for some reason, still alive and well. I thought of my mother's long blonde hair tickling my face as a baby and her bright green eyes shining at me. Her smile filled her whole face. I thought of my father with his short black hair and brilliant blue eyes looking at me in my mother's warm arms. His smile somehow filled even more of his face. A small tear ran down my cheek.

"Open your eyes class," Mrs. Blackwood whispered to all of us. I opened them slowly, letting them get used to the bright autumn sun. I looked at the rock piece in my hand and almost started crying even more than I had. It was my mother and my father in perfect detail before they died. They held the hands of a little stone five year old me in the same amount of detail. My eyes could no longer hold back my tears and my cheeks became wet with the happy sadness falling from them.

Jake looked over at me and saw what I had made. He looked me in the eyes and put his hand on my shoulder and I placed mine on top of his and gave him a smile through my silent tears. I looked at what Jake had made and saw Sarah, Noah, himself, and I. I put my hand out and he handed it to me. We were all smiling, Noah was kissing Sarah's cheek and Sarah was holding Jake's hand. I looked at me and saw that I was leaning my head on Jake's shoulder with his arm across my shoulders. I smiled at Jake once again. I felt so happy at that moment. I forgot all my worries. I felt like everything was going to be ok. That bubble was popped by the teacher telling us that class was over. I stood up and with Jake by my side. We walked back in and I went to my last class of the day.

Chapter 10

My last class of the day was spell casting. Jake dropped me off by the door and reluctantly went to his own classroom. I walked in and saw a generic classroom setup. It had a few rows of desks—only nine desks in total, and they were facing a chalkboard at the front. There was a desk in the corner where the teacher sat. In the back half of the room there was a pool, a pile of dirt and rocks, and a torch. I went and sat at one of the three desks in the middle row. When everyone arrived, only five including me, the teacher stood up and started talking.

"Good afternoon students," he said dully, "I am Mr. Brown and welcome to Spell casting." We all looked at him waiting to see what he would say next. He didn't say anything else for a good minute.

"This class is basically a place to practice your spells and what not, pretty much the mage world's version of a study hall, so go crazy. I don't care, just don't hurt yourselves and don't bother me," he said, sounding bored as he grabbed a book and sat at the desk. We all got up and moved around the room. I decided against practicing fire and went towards the pool. I had struggled with water earlier in class, so I wanted to get better. I made little droplets that I slowly grew bigger and bigger. One of the other girls in the class came over and practiced water with me. She was an elf with white-blonde hair and fair skin.

"Hi, I'm Katie," she said.

"Selene," I replied. We practiced for a little longer and then we started to get bored, so Katie decided to throw a small droplet of water at me. It hit me square on the forehead and splashed my face. I looked at her in shock and sent a slightly larger droplet of water at her for revenge. We went back and forth making bigger and bigger balls of water. We threw water at each other until Mr. Brown came over and told us to knock it off. We were drenched by that time, but I used the spell I learned from my parent's books to dry us both off.

"How are you doing that?" she asked. I had removed the water from her clothes and put the water back in the pool.

"I read a lot of spell books before I came here and I used this one all the time back home whenever it rained," I told her.

"Wow," she said as she looked at herself completely dry. Then I dried myself off. A phone rang and Mr. Brown answered it.

"Selene, you need to go to Dean Autumn's office," he said. Everyone looked at me as if I had done something wrong. Katie gave me a sad look.

"Good luck," she said to me, as I grabbed my stuff and left. I felt like a spectacle on display. I opened my map and it showed me the way to Dean Autumn's office.

The elevator opened to the same place it had before when I had gone looking for the cafeteria the day before.

"This has to be about what happened in fire class today," I thought. I was really nervous and my hands started shaking the closer I got to the door. I knocked on it, not really wanting to. I just wanted to run back to the elevator and into my room.

"Come in," a voice said through the door. I opened the door. The office was white with pillars creating a hallway-like structure that led to Dean Autumn sitting at a massive white stone desk.

"Ah Selene, please have a seat," she said while gesturing to the seat in front of the desk. I walked over to her, sat down and just stared at her. Today she was wearing a light gray suit that matched her eyes.

"Do you know why you are here?" she asked.

"I can think of many reasons as to why I am here, so I will let you tell me," I told her.

"We are here to discuss your strange happenings with fire. Your counselor Pyro told me about your test and not even a day later you almost go jumping into the fire pit in your fire class. I called you here to see if we can solve this issue," she said sternly.

"How do we solve it?" I asked. A feeling of dread started building in my stomach.

"Well it can be simply putting you into a special class or giving you detention for substance abuse. So I will have you tested for substances and if the results are negative then I will personally retest you in fire and see what I make of it," she said. I started getting nervous.

"So, Selene, are you on any substances?" she asked looking directly at me. I sensed someone else in the room and out of the corner of my eye I saw a mentalist standing almost behind me. They had their power on the edge of my mind making sure I didn't lie.

"No," I told her. After a minute she spoke.

"Well the mentalist says you're telling the truth so on to the test," she said and snapped her fingers. A person came in and placed an unlit candle on her desk. She looked at me and said,

"Do what you did for your test." So I did. I placed my fingertips on the wick and squeezed them together, picturing fire as I did. I snapped them off the wick and a small blue flame appeared as it had before. "Interesting," I heard Dean Autumn say. I looked at the fire as I did when I took my test. I felt the drawing and I went into the trance not able to resist its call. Autumn was still watching me as I put my hand into the flames. They were warm, but they didn't burn. I heard a voice in my head say, "Call on me."

I did as it said and called on the fire, but not the one in front of me, the fire inside me. The fire left the wick of the candle and was just around my hand now. I turned my hand palm up and the fire shot to the ceiling. Autumn quickly put out my fire with water magic. She looked at me stunned. I just looked at the place where the fire once was, my hand still in the air. The fire was gone from the wick. I missed it and without touching it, lit up the wick. The small blue flame appeared once again. Dean Autumn quickly put it out and took the candle away from me. She looked over at me. I just kept looking at where the fire was.

"Selene, can you hear me?" she asked. I nodded yes, but couldn't say a word, something wouldn't let me.

"Ok, I want you to try and make fire out of nothing," she said. I finally found my voice, but it didn't sound like my voice. It was childish and sounded very far away.

"But fire can't be made out of nothing," I said with the voice.

"Just try," she said calmly. So I did. I reached into the fire inside of me and brought it out. I was still in a trance-like state. I wasn't thinking, it was as if my body was being controlled by someone else. I saw a small flame appear and the more of my fire I added the bigger it grew.

"That's enough," she said quietly when I had a basketball sized flame in my hand. I stopped and brought the fire back into me. I watched as it flowed into my hand and disappeared, but it was still in me.

"What did you feel?" She asked.

"The fire inside me," I said.

"What fire?" she asked.

"The fire of my anger, my sadness, of my loss," I answered her.

"What loss?" she asked me.

"Death took them all in their hands and the loss became a fire that burned on my restrained anger and sadness," I told her, by now hot tears were rolling down my cheeks, but I felt nothing.

"Who did death claim from you?" she asked. I looked at her still in my trance. She had tears in her eyes too.

"My parents," I whispered. Then I broke out of the trance. I shook my head and looked at her clearly since I started the test.

"I'm sorry," she said and reached across the desk and grabbed my hand loosely.

"Can I go now?" I asked her. My voice had returned to normal thankfully, but I just wanted to go and lie down in my bed.

"Not just yet. I think for the safety of everyone that you have private classes for fire," she said. I wasn't mad at her for her decision and this way I couldn't hurt anyone.

"Ok," I told her.

"Good, I'll send your new schedule to you later. Now you go and rest. Have a good afternoon," she said.

I got up and left. When I got back to my room I fell onto the bed and was asleep before my head hit the pillow.

Chapter 11
Dean Autumn

That meeting did not go as expected. I thought that Selene might secretly using Ash, a drug used to improve one's ability with fire (highly addictive though), but she wasn't. She said that she was calling on the fire inside her—but what did that mean? No one should be able to do what she can do. At least no one at her age and anyone who can is already dead or very old and can't spare the magic to do so. I had no idea what was going on, but to distract myself I got to work on her new schedule. Let's see who would be a good teacher for her. Mr. Davis isn't trained enough, as is Mr. Stevens, Mrs. Smith, and Mrs. Wilson. Mr. Jackson might be able to handle her but he has a class during that block. I searched through the names of all the fire teachers and then I found the perfect teacher.

"Of course why didn't I think of her before," I said out loud. Maybe she could figure out what was happening here. I called her up and she agreed with much reluctance. She really liked her free time. I printed out a copy of Selene's new schedule and gave it to my assistant.

"Give this to Selene Woods at dinner please," I told the assistant.

"Yes ma'am," the assistant said and ran off to the dining hall. I watched her go, still wondering about Selene.

Selene

I woke to a knocking on my door. It was more of a frantic pounding than knocking. I quickly got up and opened the door.

"Selene—thank goodness! I was worried about you," Irene said in the doorway.

"Why were you worrying about me?" I asked, confused.

"You weren't at dinner and students were talking about an accident in a fire class. Then you weren't answering your door and then I didn't know what to think," she said.

"Wait a minute, did I miss dinner?" I asked. I figured word would have spread about what happened in fire class.

"No, it's happening right now. I came up when I didn't see you," she said.

"Ok, let's go then," I said stepping out of my room and closing the door.

"Alright—let's go," she said and we headed off to the Dining Hall.

"Just curious, what were you doing in your room?" she asked.

"Sleeping," I told her. She sighed and we continued walking.

I got my plate and sat with Sarah and the gang.

"Where have you been?" Sarah asked.

"Well you know that fire thing that happened today?" I asked.

"How could we forget," Noah said sarcastically.

"Well my teacher reported it to Dean Autumn and..."

"Dean Autumn? You got sent to her office?!" Sarah exclaimed.

"Yes, anyway, she had me do the test again except she didn't stop me when I put my hand in the fire," I said.

"What happened?" Jake asked quickly, picking up my hands and looking at them.

"I'm fine. I was able to call the fire to me but it was like I had to ask it for permission. Then my fire joined it and I basically made a bonfire in my hand," I told them, confused by Jake's concern.

"So, what's going to happen now?" Sarah asked.

"I'm getting private lessons with a teacher for everyone's safety," I said.

"Which teacher?" Noah asked. Just then a woman came over to our table.

"I'm looking for Selene Woods," she said.

"That's me," I told her and she handed me a folded piece of paper and left.

"What is it?" Jake asked. I opened it.

"It's my new schedule," I told them, "Looks like my new fire teacher is Mrs. Mitchell." Sarah spat out her water in shock. She spluttered and coughed. Finally she got herself together.

"Mrs. Mitchell is the greatest fire mage in the whole school!" Sarah said excitedly.

"Yeah and the toughest," Noah added.

"How do you know? You never even had her," Sarah said.

"She's kind of, my aunt," Noah said sheepishly.

"WHHAATT!!!" Sarah yelled. People looked over at us.

"It's not that big of a deal. Everyone on that side of my family is a fire mage," Noah whispered.

"But you could have introduced us. I want to meet her!" Sarah complained. They went on like this for five minutes back and forth until Noah finally agreed to take her to meet his aunt.

"Do you want me to finish with why I have to have private lessons with her?" I asked.

"Of course," Jake said.

"It's less telling and more showing," I said. I stuck out my hand, made sure no one was looking, and found the fire inside. Just like before, when I channeled it a flame appeared. I made it grow a little but not so big I couldn't control it. It was about the size of a candle flame. Then I put it out.

"That is so cool," Sarah said after a moment of silence. "How did you do that?"

"Well something in my past caused me to bottle up my anger and sadness and other emotions. Those emotions created a spark inside me and the more I held it in the brighter and stronger it got," I told her, "At least that's what I think. I'm still trying to piece it all together."

"How long have you had it bottled up?" Noah asked.

"I'd say eleven, yeah eleven years," I told them.

"What? That's crazy!" Sarah exclaimed.

"Yeah that is really insane. What in your life happened to make you like this?" Noah asked.

"I don't like to say," I said. Jake looked at me. He knew and it was only because I was vulnerable and he had cracked me open. How could I have been so ignorant? How could I have let my guard down so easily? He wanted to tell them, I could read it all over his face.

"You can tell them. I don't want to," I told Jake.

"Wait—you knew and you never told me? You were supposed to tell me why she looked broken," Sarah said.

"It's a very private thing and I wanted Selene's permission before I told anyone else," Jake said. I looked at him and smiled. He was really going to do that for me.

"So, spill dude, what happened to her?" Noah asked. Jake opened his mouth and I covered my ears. I couldn't hear this again. It was bad enough when I told it. I watched Jakes lips move to form those dreadful words. I saw the reaction on Noah's and Sarah's faces. I saw them look at me with shock, then pity. When their lips stopped moving, I removed my hand from my ears and the sounds around me flooded back.

"Please don't look at me like that," I said. They were still making their pitiful faces.

"Don't tell anyone, promise?" I asked them.

"I promise," Sarah said.

"Me too," Jake said.

"Your secrets are safe with me Selene," Noah said.

"Thanks guys," I replied. The bell rang and I walked happily back to my room for more sleep.

Chapter 12

I woke up before the first bell and took a shower. I needed to wash away the feelings of dread and unease on my mind. The water felt nice running down my back. I practiced my water magic while I was in there for entertainment. I stopped some of the droplets in mid-air and let them fall again. It was an effortless process by the end. I got out and dried myself off using more water magic. The process was that you removed the water on your body and hair by grouping it together. Then you could lift it off and send the water wherever you wanted. I got dressed—this time in a gray tank top and black leggings. I put my white hair up into a messy bun and put on a pair of sneakers. For the final touch, I grabbed my mom's old black cardigan and put it on. I grabbed my bag and staff and went to breakfast.

Breakfast was more or less the same. Sarah and Noah made lovey looks and acted like most couples act. Jake and I tried to figure out what the fire meant but I wasn't into it. My first and second classes were much like yesterday. We made balls of air and passed them to each other. Then we learned a few more new fighting moves in physical combat. Then it was time to go and see Mrs. Mitchell for the first time.

I walked down the fire wing in the school with my map opened in my hand. I saw all of the intricate symbols that represent fire on the walls. They resonated with warmth that could comfort a person, even on the coldest of nights. I found her door at the end of the hall. It was closed so I politely knocked. A thin woman with silver dusted red hair answered the door.

"You must be Selene Woods," said Mrs. Mitchell.

"Yep, that's me," I replied standing awkwardly in the doorway.

"Well, don't just stand there. Come in and take a seat on the floor," she said rudely. I did as she said ignoring the tone of voice and tried to act as nicely as I could. The room was a dirt cave with an unlit firepit in the center. Her desk was metal and in the corner of the room. Mrs. Mitchell closed the door and it disappeared. I began to get the feeling that I was trapped in here until she let me out.

"Dean Autumn seems to think that you are worthy of my teachings. The thing is, you are a first year with no background of interest, no known family, and you somehow have these amazing abilities that no one has seen since the first mages. Now personally I think you are a fraud and can't do the simplest thing and just faked your way here because you wanted to be taught by me like everyone else here. I will prove you wrong. You don't want to be taught by me and I will find out whether what you claim is truth or lies," she said. With each word I wanted at the same time to shrink away from her and punch her in the face. I didn't want her to win, so I looked at her silently waiting for instructions.

"Now what we do first is the rules. I will inspect your bag every class until I can fully believe you and once done I will place your bag in my desk and lock it in there. Secondly, no being late. If you're late, you have to stay for an hour after dinner to make it up. My final rule is do as I say and no more no less. Do you understand?" she asked. I was a little torn up at having my bag searched but I nodded my head in agreement.

"Good, now give me your bag. While I search it I want you to light the fire and no, you won't be given matches or a fire tool. You'll have to make it yourself out of nothing," she said. I handed her my bag and turned to the fire pit. I blocked out the sound of her going through my bag. I went into the fire inside me and asked its permission to be used. When I felt it agree I released the fire into my hand, which I placed on a log inside the fire pit. The fire traveled to my hand and on to the log. The log caught fire and soon caught the others on fire in a cascading effect and soon there was a blazing fire in front of me. Mrs. Mitchell had stopped going through my bag and put it in her desk drawer and looked up.

"How did you do that?" she asked curiously, yet still angrily. I guess that meant I was supposed to fail that test.

"I placed my hand on a log and sent the fire to it," I told her.

"I guess you might belong here after all," she muttered under her breath thinking I couldn't hear her. She blew the fire out using air magic. Then she came and sat beside me.

"Do it again?" she asked, this time with more curiosity than anger. I repeated my actions and once again there was a blazing fire in less than a minute.

"This is amazing. I've never seen anything like this. How do you do it?" She asked softly. I decided to tell her the truth.

"It comes from within. Fire seems to resist me unless I ask for its permission to be used, but to do that it must call me. That's what happened in my last fire class and in Dean Autumn's office except it called me too hard and I couldn't break away from it," I told her.

"Ok, but how does that allow you to create fire?" she asked, a little frustrated.

"It comes from my fire inside. I call on it and channel it to where I want it to go and there is fire," I said.

"Where does your fire come from?" she asked. I took a deep breath and said

"I'm not 100% sure, but I think it comes from my emotions. I hid them away from myself with other bad parts of me, so I couldn't feel them. Then it slowly became a fire inside me over time, raging and wanting to be let out."

She looked at me speechless and sat next to me.

"Why did you do that?" she asked quietly.

"Something happened to me when I was little and it broke me. I feel that it's my fault, like I let them down, but there was nothing I could do," I said. At this point I felt my fire inside call to me and I went to its warm embrace. It was like a warm hug.

"What happened?" Mrs. Mitchell asked.

"I saw my parent's dead one morning," I said wrapped in my fire more. I closed my eyes and let it surround me. I started disconnecting from the world. I heard Mrs. Mitchell say something, but I just shut her out and went deeper into my fire. I felt a pull on my shoulders, it pulled me slightly from my fire but I went right back in. It was so nice and it understood my pain. I felt a cold splash of water on my back, but it had no effect. I don't know how long I was there, but all I wanted was the warm embrace of my fire. But I began to feel a new, yet familiar warm grasp as someone put their arms around me.

I came out of my fire slowly into the warmth of their arms and looked up with my eyes still closed. When I finally opened them I saw Jake with his arms wrapped around me. His eyes were closed and he held me tightly in his grasp. I brought my hand to his face and he opened his eyes. When he saw me he hugged me even tighter. His actions surprised me

"I was afraid we lost you," he said. I looked around and saw that I was in the infirmary again on one of the white sheeted twin beds. Jake sat behind me with me in his lap.

"How did I get here?" I asked, sitting up quickly.

"Mrs. Mitchell called the infirmary and someone brought a wheelchair and wheeled you back here. They said you didn't want to leave the room," Jake said.

"How long have I been like this?" I asked, removing myself from him and facing him.

"Three hours," Jake replied reluctantly, "the nurses all thought you were going to die. You've been running a high fever the whole time." I looked at Jake to see what he would say next. He got up and stood beside the bed.

"You promised me nothing like this would happen again Selene. Why did you break your promise?" He asked.

"I can't always control this, but I'm getting better. My emotions just overwhelmed me this time and I was already using my fire before that happened. I'll try harder to make sure nothing like this happens again," I told him.

"Ok, and please do. I...I care about you Selene," he stuttered. I looked at him stunned. Without another word, Jake turned and quickly left.

I laid back down and was alone with the nurses who danced between patients like bees dancing from flower to flower. I couldn't do anything but think over what Jake had said to me. One of the nurses came to check on me from time to time.

"We should keep a bed open for you Ms. Woods," she joked. I wasn't in a joking mood and she quickly turned away.

I was released late that evening. I had missed dinner so I went into my dorm to eat some of the food I packed. When I walked in, Irene ran up to me, with her blonde hair streaming behind her, and gave me a big hug.

"I was so worried about you," she said.

"Really?" I asked, confused.

"Of course I was. Without you things would be really boring around here. I grabbed you a plate from dinner," she said and ran over to our kitchen and handed me a plate from the Dining Hall. I held it, but no food came.

"Oh here let me do the spell," Irene said and muttered a few words. Delicious smelling steamed zucchini and carrot arose as well as equally delicious smelling rabbit chops.

"Thank you Irene," I said. I sat at one of the couches and ate like a wolf. I was so hungry. Irene and I talked for hours about random gossip that she knew. Eventually even Irene grew bored or tired, I'm not sure which. She went off to bed and I thought I'd better go to bed as well. It had been a long and tiring day.

Chapter 13

Two days of classes went by more or less the same. Actually everything was the same. We perfected all of the techniques we had learned in every class, except fire class. There I learned how to control my fire better and how to channel it. I was of course banned from doing any fire magic outside of class for obvious reasons.

I got better acquainted with Katie in spell casting class and we became friends. She was really interesting. Like me she had grown up in a forest but, unlike me, with people and her family. I didn't tell her about my past though and she never asked about it. I think she could sense that it was a touchy subject.

At last Friday came, the day of the tournament for physical combat. I was antsy in intro to air and accidentally hit Sarah with a ball of wind. I was yelled at, but I apologized and we played around for the rest of class. When class was finally over, I got out of the class as fast as possible and went to the gym. It looked very different from the last time. It now had a big mat at the center with strings wrapping around the outside. It looked like those wrestling rings that I had read about in one of my books. The bleachers were pulled out ready for people to sit on them. The coaches stood on the mat waiting for the students to gather round. I walked over and after a few more students joined Coach Blood began to speak:

"Welcome students to your first tournament. There will be one of these every unit and many teachers bring classes down to watch, so do your best. This will be graded. Now go and get changed in the locker rooms."

Two doors appeared on the side of the gym when she said locker rooms. One was labeled girls and the other boys. I went into the girls' room and found myself in a small room. It had white walls and a white tiled floor. One large locker stood in the corner and a bench was on the side of the room. A sign on the back of the door read

This is your personal changing room
You may decorate it however you like
Please clean at the end of the year

I went over to the only locker in the room and opened it. Inside there was a close fit tank top with a pair of fitted pants and tennis sneakers.

"What color would you like to be today?" a voice asked.

"Who said that?" I jumped back startled.

"Me, I'm your locker mate; I will help you with any issues with your locker. To get started what color would you like to be?" it asked in a chirpy voice.

"What colors are there?" I asked back.

"Any color that isn't already taken," it replied.

"White then," I said.

"Locking in your color, color now chosen, applying color," it said. Then the outfit in the locker turned from a semi transparent color to a bright white.

"Cool," I said.

"Would you like assistance getting dressed?" the locker asked.

"No thank you," I said, grabbing the outfit. I quickly got changed and grabbed my staff from my bag. I then tied my hair up into a bun, so that it wouldn't impede my fighting by getting into my face. Then I placed my school clothes and my bag into the locker.

"Keep these safe for me," I told the locker.

"Of course," it chirped happily, "now you must wait here until you first fight."

"Thank you again, Uh, what's your name?" I asked.

"Huh. No one has ever asked for a name from me before. Yay! I'm Eliza," she said happily.

"Nice to meet you Eliza," I said, "I'm Selene." I talked with Eliza until I heard a knock on the door.

"Selene you're up next," I heard Coach Blood say.

"Goodbye Eliza," I said, grabbing my staff.

"Have a good time Selene," Eliza said. I went to the door and when Coach Blood came back, I left the room.

I looked around and saw the bleachers were half-filled with students. There was now a board with brackets on it. It looked like seven matches had happened already and about eight, not including mine, were still to happen. I never realized how many students were in this class. I walked into the ring where Coach Swift stood. He was holding a microphone in one hand.

"Welcome next contestants, students we have Nicholas Miller on one side and Selene Woods on the other," he said. I heard calls from the stands and saw Jake and Sarah sitting there clapping for me. I smiled at them.

"Settle down students we have a lot more battles to get through," Swift said. I looked at Nicholas on the opposite side of the mat. He was thin with mousy brown hair and wore thick framed glasses. I started making a plan of attack in my head.

"Contestants ready yourselves," Swift said. I got into my stance. My feet shoulders length apart, my side facing Nicholas, and my staff across the front side of my body with my right hand at the top third, palm facing up, and my left hand on the back third palm down. Nicholas did the most ridiculous thing ever and placed his staff in front of him with both hands on top of each other on one end and the other end on the mat. He then proceeded to lift one leg till his foot was at his knee. He looked like a weird crane.

"Fight," Swift said. I waited to see what Nicholas would do. He got into a different stance which was a lunge forward with his staff being held at the back with both hands. He shuffled forward and swung at me like he held a baseball bat. I dodged easily and went up to him, swung at his legs and my staff caught his back foot and unbalanced him. I proceeded to hit him across the chest. He landed on his back and I pointed my staff at his neck. This was the sign of defeat that was standard in duels. The whole match had only taken a minute. Nicholas looked at me stunned and embarrassed.

"Good try," I whispered nicely to him. He gave me a small smile and I removed my staff, twirling it, and placed it at my side. He got up and grabbed his own staff and left with his head down.

"And we have a winner for this first round," Swift said. I walked back to the locker room looking back one last time at Jake and Sarah who were going crazy.

Chapter 14

I talked with Eliza in between my rounds. I asked Eliza what her favorite color was and told her mine. Mine was a tie between black and white. Eliza liked pink, a lot. She went on and on about all of the different shades of pink there are and how she liked all of them except this one color that looks more brown than pink. It was called rosewood and Eliza said that it did look like a rose had blended with a tree, but it was still gross looking. Coach Blood knocked on my door again. I got my staff and came out glad for the break from Eliza. I walked out and saw more students sitting in the stands. I looked at my opponent and this time she was female. She had short brown hair and a yellow outfit identical to mine.

"Welcome again contestants. Which of you will move on to the semi-finals?" Coach Swift asked.

"I am," my opponent shouted.

"So she's cocky," I thought and once again began strategizing.

"On this side we have the first year Selene Woods and on the other we have the second year and returning champ Mary Lewis," Swift said.

"So they wanted to give me a challenge," I thought and revised my strategy.

"Ladies get ready," Swift said. I got into the same stance as before. Mary did the same stance as me but using opposite hands to mine.

"Go," Swift shouted. Once again I waited and again my opponent made the first move. Mary stepped to the side and came at my back. I rolled forward to dodge and then back through her legs so that I was behind her. I swung at her back and made contact but she remained standing. She turned to me with fury in her eyes. She put her staff over her head and swung at my head. I tried to dodge but the tip of her staff hit my head. It hurt but I've known worse pain and fought through it.

We traded blows back and forth blocking with our staffs. Mary would jab at me and I would parry. Soon she started to tire and on her next jab I sidestepped and smacked her across the stomach. She let go of her staff in pain and doubled over. I thwacked her on the back and she fell to the ground. She rolled over to her back and saw her staff. Then she rolled onto her stomach and went for her staff. I kicked it out of her way and, as I did with Nicholas, pointed the edge of my staff at her throat. She turned over and looked up at me with surprise and then hatred.

"And we have a winner," Swift said. Everyone gasped. Sarah and Jake applauded and were the only ones to. I let Mary get up and we walked back to the locker rooms—Mary to get back into her normal clothes to watch from the stands and me to wait for the semi-finals.

I went into the locker room. I had been in the first match of this round so I was going to have to wait awhile. I meditated a bit but that ended quickly with Eliza's chipping voice. I then tried to block her out, but she has one of those voices that you just couldn't quite block out no matter how hard you tried. I gave up and tried a bit of magic but nothing I tried worked.

"Eliza, why can't I do magic here?" I asked.

"There is a magical dampener on all locker rooms so that students don't cheat before a fight," Eliza said.

"Oh, can they be turned off?" I asked curiously.

"Only by the coaches, the janitors, and Dean Autumn herself," Eliza answered.

Hmm, maybe I could figure out how to shut them down. No, it wouldn't be right, plus I could be accused of cheating. So I laid down on the bench and listened to Eliza talk.

The semi-finals began. I could hear people shouting outside the door. I soon heard the knock to call me to battle; I got ready and went out. There were even more students and the bleachers were almost filled with students and teachers. I walked up to the ring and saw my opponent. She was wearing light blue and she had long blonde hair coming down around her.

"Students and teachers, I welcome you to the Semi-final round. We have an exciting match between the first year Selene Woods and one of our other first years Linda Thompson," Coach Swift announced, "Ready." I readied myself in my usual stance and Linda put her staff horizontally across her front and placed one hand at each end facing me.

"Fight," Swift shouted. There was a roar of excitement from the crowd that soon died down as they saw that neither Linda nor I were attacking each other. We were both waiting for the other to strike.

After a minute I decided to break the tension and make a false swing. It was designed to make an opponent think that you don't know what you are doing. Linda fell for it and swatted my staff away and went to strike at my stomach. I quickly brought my staff back to my center and blocked her. She was furious.

"You are not going to win this," she spat at me angrily. Without a reply I rushed her and swept her legs out from under her. I put my staff to her throat.

"Actually I am," I said slyly. The match was over. I stood and started walking back to the locker rooms.

"And Selene Woods has won again," Swift said. I heard a cry of anger and turned to find Linda charging at me. I brought up my staff and blocked her attack. Her attacks were anger fueled and sloppy, so they were easy to dodge or parry.

I continued to do so until Linda gave up from exhaustion. It had taken her a good five minutes with everyone watching. When she finally cooled down Coach Blood ran over and walked her back to the locker rooms talking to her sternly. I went back to the locker room once she went in. I wasn't there long before I had to come out again. It was only a two minute break. I walked out to see who my next opponent was and saw Noah on the other side of the mat with his staff in hand.

Chapter 15

I looked at Noah and he looked at me. I looked into the stands at Jake and Sarah. There was disbelief in their faces.

"Now for our final match, we have Selene Woods vs. Noah Martinez," Coach Swift announced. I walked up to Coach Swift.

"May I speak with my opponent quickly?" I asked.

"I don't know why you would, but okay. Good time for me to use the bathroom," he said and ran over towards the restrooms. I went over to Noah and grabbed his sleeve and pulled him to the back of the room away from the crowd.

"What's up?" Noah asked.

"I don't want to fight you. You're my friend," I told him. He looked at me for a minute, sighed and finally said, "I don't want to fight you either but they won't just let us forfeit. There has to be a battle and there has to be a winner. I'm sorry to say this but I want to win and if that means I have to beat you then I will." He walked back to the ring without looking back at me. I watched him walk away in disbelief and soon followed him.

"Fine. If he wants a battle, I'll give him one," I muttered angrily. We got back to the mat and Coach Swift was back from the bathroom.

"Ready," he shouted and I readied myself. They were going to have to scrape Noah off the mat once I was done with him. I stared him down and he returned my stare.

"Fight," Swift shouted. Noah charged at me and I parried his staff to the side and stepped the opposite way. He came at me again this time swinging to come in contact with my side. I ducked underneath it and smacked him across the back. He rubbed the spot and turned on me with annoyance. We faced each other, staffs at our sides, in our right hands breathing hard. We charged at each other at the same time and our staffs clashed. We fought like this for a good time just trading blows and parrying.

Eventually Noah landed a blow to my stomach that made me go to my knees. He raised his staff to hit me over my head and push me down but I had my staff in both hands and put it up over my head. I blocked his attack and pushed his staff off mine. This action unbalanced him tipping him back and I used it to my advantage. I rushed him and hit him across the chest. He fell over and landed on his back. I quickly put my staff at his throat. He got onto his elbows and I pushed my staff closer to his throat. He looked me in the eyes and accepted defeat. I stood and held out my hand. He accepted it and I helped him up.

"We have a new champion this year. Congratulations to Selene Woods," Coach Swift said. Some students cheered and others booed, but there were very few boos. Jake and Sarah remained silent. I understood—on one hand one of their friends had won, but on the other their other friend had lost. I walked off the mat and back to my locker room.

"You won Selene. Congrats! I've never had a winner before," Eliza said as soon as I walked in.

"Thanks," I replied. I got back into my normal clothes, happy to be out of the tight fitting and sweaty gym clothes. I went back into the gym and saw my class, assembled in the center of the room when I came out. Students and teachers were clearing from the bleachers. I jogged over to my class to hear what the Coaches were saying.

"Good battles everyone. Your grade will reflect how well you performed in combat. Now get to your next class," Coach Blood said and the students dispersed to the doors. I turned to walk out.

"Selene, can you wait a few minutes? We want to talk with you," Coach Swift called.

"Alright," I said and walked back to them.

"You performed well today," Coach Blood complimented.

"Thank you," I said.

"Yes, and we want to congratulate you with this secret prize," Coach Swift said. He went into his office and came back with a box in his hand.

"Here it is. Just wait to open it until you get back into your dorm," Coach Swift said, placing the box in my hand.

"And before you ask, yes, Dean Autumn is ok with this. Every winner gets one. Some last but most don't," Coach Blood said with a wink.

"What is it?" I asked with a feeling they were hiding something.

"Wait and see," Coach Swift said.

I left still curious about the box. I decided to listen to the coaches, stashed it in my bag, and went to fire class. Mrs. Mitchell was probably already upset that the tournament had taken away half her class time and I didn't want to be any later.

Chapter 16

It was boring for the rest of the day. All my classes paled in comparison to the tournament. Because of the shortened class, Mrs. Mitchell decided to have an afterschool class. So after dinner I went to Mrs. Mitchell's class room.

"Hello Selene," She said once I got there.

"Hello Mrs. Mitchell," I said kind of glumly. I didn't mind having to stay with her but I wanted to open up that box.

"I thought we'd try something different tonight," She said.

"What did you have in mind?" I replied, dreading the response.

"Fire has many unique qualities, but what I want to try is prophecies. It's a little advanced, but I think you are ready for it," she said.

"Ok, so what do I have to do?" I asked.

She started explaining to me that I had to create a fire and while doing so focus on a specific aspect of the future that I wanted to know about. I thought for a moment and found something I wanted to know. Then I made a grapefruit-sized fire in my hand and thought more about the thing I wanted to know.

"Alice," I whispered into the flames. The fire started to spin in my hand faster and faster until it was a flat disk. I looked on the flat side and a picture of Alice appeared. Her mouth moved but I could hear no sound. I looked at her and saw that she was older, about 30ish. There was a tall man next to her with brown eyes and a beard. Between them was a little boy and girl. The boy couldn't be more than five and the girl no more than three. I looked at Alice again and saw that she was pregnant. Alice had always told me that she wanted a big family. I looked at Alice's face and she was smiling. Her whole family looked happy. I brought the fire back into my center and just stared out in space smiling.

"Selene," Mrs. Mitchell whispered, shaking my shoulder gently, "Are you alright?"

"I'm better than alright," I told her softly. I looked at Mrs. Mitchell and smiled at her. Then I let out a little laugh.

"You know what, I think that is the first time you've laughed since you've been in my class," Mrs. Mitchell said. She smiled too and it was one of those smiles that reached all the way to her eyes.

"You can go back to your room," Mrs. Mitchell said and handed me my bag. I looked at the clock and saw that I had only been here for 5 minutes.

"But it's not time yet," I said.

"I know. I'm letting you go early. Now go before I change my mind," she said playfully. I went to the door and turned around to face her.

"Thank you Mrs. Mitchell. Have a lovely night," I said and walked out the door.

I got back to my dorm and heard Irene's snores inside her room. I crept quietly to my room not wanting to wake her. I placed my bag on the desk and sat in the chair. It was finally time to open the mysterious box. I opened my bag and stuck my hand in and thought of the box. After a second, it materialized in my hand as this was the magic of the bag. Lifting it carefully out, I examined it. The box was small, about the size of my hand, and wooden with black scorch marks on it. On closer examination I saw that the scorch marks created symbols. There were very intricate spirals, swirls, and different shapes. It was a masterful piece. I found the lid on the box and slid in back. Smoke, or maybe it was fog, poured out from the open top.

When it died away all that was left was an egg-like object. I took the object out of the box and looked at it closely. It was a beautiful white crystal with a scale design on it. Inside was a shadow of some animal. I placed the object back into the box and saw a small sheet of paper tucked inside. I reached in and picked it up. Unfolded it, I saw some writing on the inside.

Dear Selene,

> *By winning this tournament, you have shown that you have strength and cunning. I know I said that this was a prize but no one has ever received this prize. Dean Autumn said to give this to you as a gift and, to make it look less suspicious, we decided to*

give this to you for winning the tournament. Normally it's a nice staff or something, but we think this is better. This box contains a dragon egg. If the proper steps are taken, the egg will hatch into a dragon and it will bond to you. It will protect you and keep you company. You can find the steps in the library. Dean Autumn has left a book for you there. Just tell the librarian your name and she will get it for you. Have a good time with this new companion if you succeed.

Brightest wishes,
Coach Blood and Coach Swift

PS Tell no one.

I sat back in my chair and looked at the object—it was an egg. A dragon egg! I couldn't believe it. I closed up the box and put it back in my bag to keep it safe.

"I'll go to the library tomorrow morning before breakfast," I thought. I yawned and got into my pajamas, then hung my bag on a hook, and climbed into bed falling fast asleep.

I woke before the bell to go to the library. I was excited to see what it would look like. I had been so busy with classes and my social life that I hadn't had a chance to go yet.

I walked in with my map in hand and gasped. The place was huge. There were bookshelves as far as the eye could see all filled to the brim with books. The shelves reached up to the ceilings and had to be at least two stories high. I walked down the four steps to the main floor of the library and saw balconies around the outside of the library with doors leading to unknown rooms. In front of me was a large desk stacked high with books. A woman with gray hair piled up into a messy bun sat in between the piles of books. I walked up to her, assuming that she was the librarian.

"Excuse me," I said quietly.

"Can I help you miss?" she asked looking up at me.

"Hi, I'm Selene Woods. I was told there was a book here for me," I told her a bit nervous.

"Ah, yes. I have it right here," she said and bent down to go into one of her drawers. She pulled out a long book that was relatively thin.

"Here you go," she said after she had written my name and date on the card saying that I had checked out the book.

"Thank you—have a great day," I said and left quickly. I couldn't wait to get started.

I decided to skip breakfast at the Dining Hall and ate the last of my food from home for breakfast. Then I could stay in my room to work on the hatching all day. Since it was Saturday, it was an independent study day. Same for Sundays, so I sat at my desk with my food and opened the book. A small piece of paper fell out from between the pages. I picked it up and read the note.

Selene,

I hope this note finds you well. I want to explain to you why I gave you this egg. It has been in my family for many years, gifted to us from the last dragon's own nest. There are only three others like this. A dragon can only be controlled by its mother or someone like her. Since this dragon's mother was killed in battle and her eggs were divided and given to the most powerful mage families, my family has been searching for a new owner of the egg since. I think you could be a possible owner. Your inner fire resembles that of the dragon mother. I was told of what her fire felt like and it is similar to yours. Take care of this dragon and keep it safe. On page 24 is a spell to make a dragon room in your dorm. This will be a safe place for the dragon, but keep it hidden just in case. Any other instructions you need will be in the book. I will provide food for your dragon once it is born. When you hatch the dragon please come and see me.

Brightest wishes,
Dean Autumn

I opened the book to page 24 and found the spell.

"Might as well get started. There's no use having a dragon if I can't house it," I said to myself. I walked over to a wall that was completely blank, following the book's instructions, and chanted the words of the spell calling on fire as I did so.

> *"Space is what I desire for my soon to be dragon*
> *Fire I call to make my desires true,"*

Fire escaped from my hand and burned away a portion of the wall. After the flames went out I saw the paint had melted and formed the same symbols as on the wooden box. The wood underneath the paint had been burnt and scorch marks could now be seen, same as the box. It was beautiful looking. I spotted a black circular door knob set into the left side of the door. I went and grabbed it with my left hand, quickly removing it.

"Ouch!" I yelled.

The door knob was scalding hot. I had never been burnt before so this was a whole new experience. I looked at my hand and it started turning really red and hurt a lot. But as the redness started to fade, I saw a black burn mark in the shape of a dragon curled up. It looked almost like a brand. My hand started to hurt less and I read the rest of the spell instructions.

Make sure you open the door right away so the door knob can give you your mark. It will hurt, but it is necessary. The dragon will see the mark and think of you as its mother. It's also the only way to open the door.

"Thanks for the warning about that, book," I thought angrily. I put the book back on my desk and sat on my bed. I looked closer at my hand tracing the mark left by the dragon door. I was going to have to hide this. I didn't want anyone else to know about this until the hatching was complete. I went into my closet and saw my mom's old pair of black silk dress gloves. I grabbed the left one and put it on. It was a little loose around my upper arm but it hid my palm. I went out into the common room to clear my head.

Chapter 17

Irene was sitting on one of the couches scrolling through her phone. She looked up at the sound of my door opening.

"Hey," she said, "I didn't see you this morning. Are you alright?"

"I'm fine. I just slept in and ate in my room," I lied quickly closing my door. I didn't really want Irene to know what I was doing.

"Ok, well some of the girls and I are going to town. You want to come?" Irene asked.

"Not really, I have some things to do," I said.

"Oh come on, you never do anything fun. Lighten up a bit," she said annoyingly.

"Fine," I said quickly, wanting her to stop pestering me.

"Great, go get into something fashionable and meet me out here in five," She said and went to her room. I walked slowly back to mine wishing I hadn't agreed. I didn't really like the looks of Irene's friends. I walked in and saw the mess that I had made with all of the dragon preparation and decided to first clean up. I put the book on the shelf and the box holding the egg in my desk drawer. I looked at the door and sighed.

How was I ever going to hide that? Then it hit me. I found one of my dad's old spell books of illusions. I found the camouflage illusion that would hide the door and make it look like a normal wall. I quickly performed the spell and I watched as the door slowly disappeared. I could still tell that it was there but if someone wasn't looking intentionally at it they wouldn't be able to tell the difference. I also did a quick clean up spell to tidy things up.

I went into my closet and tried to find something "fashionable" as Irene said. I put on a tight fit black t-shirt that hung low in the back and a pair of black skinny jeans. I then put my hair up in a messy bun and went out to see if it was up to Irene's standards.

When I walked out Irene looked at me and said, "We are taking a trip back to your closet to see what you have. I am going to pick out an outfit for you and you are going to wear it."

"Fine," I said, not really caring. Irene went into my closet and after a minute came out with my white crop top that I wore when I was sunbathing.

"Your jeans will have to do, but this is great. Why do you not wear this more?" she asked.

I ignored her and went into the bathroom and changed. When I came out Irene smiled.

"There—isn't that better? now all we need are shoes and some makeup," she exclaimed.

"Well there are shoes in the closet but I don't own any makeup," I said. It wasn't an important thing that I thought needed, way back when I had gathered everything I could from my old house.

"Really! Oh well, we'll just have to do without it," She said going into my closet once again. She came out with a pair of heeled ankle boots. It had been years since I had worn them. The last time was when Alice's parents had invited me over for dinner for the first time.

"These are the only heels that you have, so they'll have to do. Now hurry up and put them on and take off that glove. It ruins the whole look," she said.

"I'll put the shoes on but I can't take the glove off. I accidentally burned myself this morning and I'm trying to keep it covered," I half-lied.

"Alright, fine. Just put the other one on then," she said and walked out of my room. I quickly put on my shoes and grabbed the other glove. I followed her out.

We met up with her friends at the front gate. Irene quickly introduced me to her friends Lauren, Sam, Julia, and Margaret. They just looked at me and in unison said, "Whatever," and started gossiping about who liked who and who was dating who.

After a few minutes of just standing there. I leaned over to Irene and asked, "What are we waiting for?" She looked at me and smiled as a black van with red and orange actual flames on it came towards us. It pulled up to the front gate and Irene's friends started getting in.

"Who is this?" I asked Irene.

"Don't worry about it, now come on," Irene said grabbing my arm and pulling me into the crowded van. I found a seat in the back and tried to just hide away. There were four guys from a neighboring school who had picked us up and were apparently Irene's friend's boyfriends. We drove for a while with music blasting and soon arrived at a nearby town. Once we entered the town the flames on the van just turned to normal old paint. It was actually cool looking. Soon we pulled up to a club.

"Irene," I whisper.

"What's wrong now Selene?" Irene asked.

"You never told me we would be going to a club," I said.

"It's fine. It's just dancing and eating and just a little drinking," Irene said.

"What? Irene I'm not really comfortable with this," I said.

"It's ok. Calm down and just have some fun," Irene said and practically pulled me into the club.

Inside it was dark with flashing lights from lasers and other lights. The whole building pulsed with the music. I couldn't hear myself think. I followed Irene deeper into the club and saw round tables and chairs surrounding a square dance floor full of teens and young adults. Most were drunk. Irene's friends sat at a table in the corner while their older boyfriends got them some alcoholic drinks.

"'So what do you want to do first?" Irene asked. I wanted to go back to the dorms, but instead I said very unconvincingly, "Let's dance."

"Now you're getting it," Irene said and pulled me onto the dance floor. I just shuffled awkwardly while Irene had somehow made a dance circle and was in the center dropping low to the floor and coming back up again swinging her hips with some strange guy. I left her to dance and I found an empty table in the corner away from Irene's friends. I watched everyone laughing and having fun. Irene was dancing like crazy with a different strange guy and her friends were guzzling down booze. I stood up and sighed. I shouldn't have come. It was a mistake. I started walking to the door when someone grabbed my hips. I turned around to give the person a piece of my mind and saw Jake looking at me.

Chapter 18

I hugged Jake when I realized it wasn't some pervert and then pulled back realizing what I had done.

"Jake. What are you doing here? Not that I'm not happy you're here," I asked.

"I heard that there was a club around here. I used to go to them all the time back home. This one's pretty good I must admit," he said, "The real question is what are you doing here?"

"Irene dragged me here to party with her friends," I told him.

"That sucks. They are no fun to party with. They just get drunk and try to hook up with any guy they see," he said.

"But some of them have boyfriends," I told him confused.

"My point exactly. Hey why don't we get out of here and go somewhere fun?" he asked.

"Yes, please. Get me out of here as soon as possible," I said and we walked out of the gloom of the club into the bright sunshine.

"So what do you want to do first?" Jake asked.

"What is there to do?" I asked.

"Lots," he said.

"How about some lunch first?" I asked.

"Ok, I heard about a few places from my roommate. I'll take you to them," he said and started walking down the street. We stopped in front of a diner a few blocks away from the club.

"People say that this place has the best food in town," Jake said. He opened the door for me and I walked in. Inside was a retro style diner. It had black and white checkered tile floors and mustard yellow walls. There were red booths by the windows and a bar on the side. Jake took a seat at an empty booth and I sat across from him. Then a waitress came up to us. She looked in her late twenties and had long blonde hair tied up in a pile on her head.

"Hi, I'm Chloe. I'll be your waitress today. Here are your menus and can I get the two of you anything to drink?" she asked.

"I'll just have a glass of water," I said.

"Coke for me please," Jake said politely.

"Sure thing. Let me know when you're ready to order," Chloe said. I looked at the menu and saw burgers, sandwiches, breakfast, soups, salads, and more.

"Wow!" I exclaimed.

"I know. What to choose," Jake said. I looked at the menu a little longer and decided what I was going to have. I looked up at Jake and he looked like he was done deciding. Chloe came back with our drinks and placed them on the table and gave us two straws.

"Have you decided what you want?" she asked.

"Yes," Jake said and Chloe took out an order sheet, "I'll have a cheeseburger with tomato, lettuce and pickles with fries."

"I'll have a grilled cheese sandwich," I said when Jake was done.

"That comes with soup and salad. What soup would you like?" Chloe asked.

"Um....clam chowder," I said, seeing it on the menu.

"Ok and what dressing on the salad?" she asked.

"Italian," I said. It was the only dressing I knew.

"Great, I'll be out with your food in a minute," she said and left. Then I realized something, I had no money.

"Jake," I whispered.

"Yes?" he asked.

"I don't have any money," I said.

"Don't worry about it, my parents are loaded," he said.

"Really? What do they do for a living?" I asked.

"Well my mom is a much respected healer at a well known hospital, for mages of course, and my dad owns his own company. He sells a candy brand that when you eat them; they explode in your mouth. There are different kinds like chocolate, hard candy, gummies, and a lot more. It's like the most popular candy ever made in the mage world," Jake bragged.

"I've never had one," I said sheepishly.

"Really, I'll have to give you a box when we get back to school. My dad gave me a few for school," Jake said.

"Thanks," I replied, "Hey, how did you know how Irene and her friends party?" He didn't get to answer though because just then the waitress came back with our food and we started eating.

Chapter 19

Jake gave me a ride back to school. We stopped at the club so I could tell Irene I was leaving. She didn't want me to go but I went anyway. I had a dragon to hatch.

Jake walked me to his room and gave me a box of candies.

"Try one," he said. I opened the box and ate one of the candies. It was hard at first but as it sat on my tongue I heard a pop and a wave of delicious flavor rolled over my tongue. It was sweet yet sour with a refreshing lemon after taste. Then it was gone.

"That was amazing!" I exclaimed.

"Right!" he said, "The best part is that they don't go into your digestive system so you basically have your favorite flavors with no consequences."

"These are so cool. Your dad must be really amazing," I said.

"Yeah he is, at least when I see him that is," he said sadly. We started walking down the hall back to my room.

"What do you mean?" I asked.

"Well, my parents are both really busy with their jobs, so I don't see them a lot. Most of the time I see one or the other, rarely ever do I see them together," he said.

"That must be hard," I said.

"It can be, especially because they are also both on the Council and that takes up any of their free time. But you had it harder with what happened to you," he said.

"I'd rather not bring it up," I said, wincing inside.

"Oh of course," he said apologetically, "I wasn't thinking."

"No, no it's okay. I just don't want to think of it. Now that you know, just try not to bring it up," I replied.

"Alright," he said. We arrived at my door and I looked at him.

"Thanks for taking me away from that club. I had a fun time with you," I said and opened the door.

"Do you mind if I come in? I know Irene isn't here and I just want to spend more time with you," he asked. I looked at him stunned. On one hand I wanted to let him in but on the other I had a dragon to try and hatch. I wasn't supposed to tell anyone about it, but I trusted Jake more than I've trusted anyone before.

"Ok, but I have to do some work," I said.

"Ok. I understand," he replied. We walked in and I led him to my room.

"Nice," he said, "You have a lot of books."

"Yeah, they are mostly my parents' spellbooks," I said.

"So what work do you have to do?" he asked as he sat at my desk.

"This," I replied and took the dragon book off my shelf.

"So you're studying what you would do if you had a dragon's egg?" Jake asked confused.

"Not if I have a dragon egg," I said and took the box off the shelf. I opened it and stood next to Jake and showed him.

"Incredible! Do you know how rare these are? How did you even get one?" he asked.

"Believe it or not, Dean Autumn," I said.

"Really."

"I know, right? It came as a shock to me too. But her family has been protecting it for generations—ever since the last dragon fell," I said.

"I remember that. It was during the last mage war. Our champion, Alfred Anorak, was the greatest mage ever. He had this great dragon that he was bonded to. They were an unstoppable force but their enemy, dark mage Douglas Donahue, had his own secret weapon—a dragon killer. No one knows what it looked like. All anyone saw was a bright flash in the sky. When the sky returned to normal the dragon fell to earth dead and when a dragon dies, so does its companion and vice versa. Of course this all happened hundreds of years ago," Jake said.

"Wow—how do you know all of this?" I asked.

"I had private tutors until I came here. My parents wanted to make sure I knew my stuff," he said.

"So did they ever find the weapon?" I asked.

"No. That's what is weird about the whole thing. After the flash Douglas and his entire army disappeared. Some say the weapon killed them. Others say that he is still alive, growing his army, waiting for when the time is right to return," Jake said creepily.

"But hey, that part is only a myth," he added with a shrug.

"Yeah," I said unsure, "Well I'm going to try and hatch this dragon."

"Cool," Jake said. I grabbed the book from the desk where Jake had placed it, sat on the desk, and started reading.

"Finished!" I exclaimed.

"Huh, What," Jake said with a start as his snores stopped. It was 6:00 pm and we had started at 1:00 pm so I understood him falling asleep. It was a thin but information filled book.

"I finished the book," I said.

"Oh good, so what do you have to do?" he asked.

"Well it says that the final stages of the hatching must happen when the moon is on fire," I said.

"Ok. Now, what does that mean?" he asked, confused. I giggled.

"It's the harvest moon because the moon is orange. Lucky for me, it's on Friday," I said.

"Ok, so what needs to be done before then?" he asked.

"The egg needs to be kept in a warm place for 13 hours straight. Then there is a tapping rhythm that is needed to tell the baby dragon that it is time to hatch—that lasts for a full two days and must be done within 24 hours after the 13 hours or the dragon will die. Finally, after two days of tapping, there are like three pages of spells that need to be chanted over the egg and other rituals," I told him.

"Doesn't seem that hard other than not getting much sleep," he said.

"Yeah well here is the hard part," I explained. "The dragon will try to hatch once the harvest moon rises but I can't let it finish until the sun rises the next day. If the dragon hatches at night, the dragon will have no fire and will die once the sun rises. I have to keep the dragon asleep. The only way to do this is to keep the egg temperature at about 1200 degrees—and the person who will own the dragon must hold the egg for the entire time."

"Ouch."

"Yeah."

"So what are you going to do?" he asked me.

"What the book says," I told him.

"But you'll get burnt," he said concerned.

"A small price to pay for the birth of a new dragon in this world. Besides, I think I have a few ways to remove most of the pain and there shouldn't be much with my weird ability with fire," I said.

"Right, I had almost forgotten about that," Jake replied.

"I'll start tomorrow with the process. There are still preparations that are needed for the dragon room," I said.

"What dragon room?" he asked. I looked at the wall and had completely forgotten about the camouflage illusion hiding the door.

"Oh right. Give me a minute to remove the illusion," I said and grabbed my dad's book on the Illusion. I found the page and disenchanted the illusion. The door slowly became more and more visible. Once it was totally visible Jake let out a whistle.

"That is quite the door," he said.

"Yeah," I said and went to open it. I grabbed the handle with my right hand and tried to open it. It wouldn't budge.

"Huh."

"What's wrong?" Jake asked.

"The door won't open," I told him and walked back to my desk and searched the dragon book for an answer.

"Oh okay, it says here that the dragon door can only be opened by the marked hand," I said.

"And what does that mean?" he asked still confused. I removed my glove from my left hand and showed him.

"Oh ouch, that looks like it hurt," he said, wincing a little.

"It did, but not anymore," I told him and I went to open the door, this time with my left hand. The door swung in easily and we walked in. I realized that this was the first time I had been in the dragon room. It was dimly lit with just the light from the door coming in. I called up a fireball and sent it to the middle of the ceiling. It illuminated the room and the gloom was lifted. On the back wall was a huge fireplace with symbols etched around it in the stone chimney. To the right was a pool of water with a fresh spring running into it. Next to that was a metal pan on which I assumed the dragon's food would be placed. The floor had bedding of some kind of material where the dragon could sleep. The whole room looked like it was a cave. On further examination, clear gemstones embedded in the cave walls glowed slightly.

"Wow," Jake said and started walking around the room. It was a large room, big enough for a growing dragon.

"So what preparations are going to be needed?" Jake asked.

"Right," I had almost forgotten in my amazement of the room. "The fireplace needs to be lit, the pan needs to be cleaned, and the bed ready for the new dragon."

"Ok, I'll get the bed ready," he said and I told him how.

"I'll go start up the fire in the fireplace," I said. I called up my fire and placed it gently on the logs that were already there. Once the fire caught on, I pulled away and brought my fire back inside.

"You're getting good at that," Jake said. I looked up and saw him watching me.

"Yeah Mrs. Mitchell's teachings have really helped me with controlling the fire," I said. I walked back over to Jake and helped him with the bed. Then I cleaned out the pan.

"All right. I think we're done," I said.

"What about the food?" he asked.

"Dean Autumn will give me some once the dragon hatches," I told Jake. We walked out of the dragon room. I closed the door and we stood in my dorm room once again.

"You can't tell anyone about this Jake. I wasn't even supposed to tell you," I said as I camouflaged the door.

"Of course I won't," Jake said and then he faced me and just looked at me.

"What?" I asked him.

"Um...It's just that I–" Jake started to say. Then I saw the clock.

"Oh shoot, its 8:15. We'd better hurry to dinner," I said. Jake gathered his things and we ran off to the Dining Hall.

Chapter 20

We walked into the normal hubbub of the dining hall with people talking and showing off. I began to notice a few tables here that were normally filled were strangely empty.

"Where is everyone?" I asked Jake.

"Either at home nearby, partying, or wreaking havoc on the nearby towns," Jake sighed. We grabbed some plates and sat down at our table. Noah was already sitting there.

"Where's Sarah?" Jake asked. I had never seen those two apart unless it was for classes.

"Her sister dragged her off for a girls' night out in town," he mumbled. We sat down and ate in silence. I realized that without Sarah we were normally quiet people.

"Hey Selene," Noah spoke up.

"Yes Noah?"

"I'm sorry about the tournament. You did great and I shouldn't have said those things," he apologized.

"Wait—what am I missing here," Jake chimed in.

"In the final round of last Friday's physical combat tournament, Noah and I fought each other."

"Um...Yeah?"

"Well I didn't want to fight him and when I told him that he basically said he was going to win even if it meant beating me to a pulp," I said.

"What?!"

"I didn't say it like that!" Noah exclaimed.

"Yeah, but you still said you were going to beat me, even if I was a friend," I retorted.

"Noah that's not cool dude," Jake said.

"I know and that's why I was apologizing. I got caught up in the heat of the moment. My entire family expects greatness from me—like all my ancestors. It can be a bit overwhelming and I can lose touch of what's important. I'm sorry. Please forgive me?" Noah begged.

"Ok, I think you've begged enough. I forgive you," I told him.

"Thank you."

The rest of dinner was uneventful. We all talked a little and finished eating. At the end of the night Noah invited us to a place called the Cavern.

"Noah, how did you get into the Cavern?!" Jake asked excitedly.

"I have my connections," he said.

"Am I the only one who has no idea what you are talking about," I said confused.

"You'll see," said Noah and pulled out a map. It looked like a school map but instead of saying where you want to go, as soon as it was open a location appeared with no instructions.

"Oh, I know where that is!" Jake exclaimed. He was really excited.

"Great, lead the way," Noah said. Jake ran off down a hallway and we chased after him.

After a half hour and three wrong turns later, we stood in front of a normal looking classroom door.

"Ok, will someone please tell me what is going on?" I was getting frustrated with a search that seemed to end at a dead end.

"I thought it would be best if I just showed you," Noah said and opened the door to anything but a normal classroom. The place was huge. There were rows of arcade games and other types of games on one side and on the other a huge pool the size of a small lake that stretched as far as the eye could see. People were swimming and playing games and just having a fun time all over. There was a drink station with multiple different fizzy drinks and bowls of candies, chips, pretzels, and more. In the center was a lounge area with lots of couches and chairs around a bonfire. The whole place looked like a stone cave with colorful gems as lights.

"Wow," I said overwhelmed. The place was stunning.

"I know, right? Welcome to Center Ark Versatile Entertaining and Relaxing Nook, but everyone just calls it the Cavern," Noah said. "Well I'm heading off to the arcade."

"I think I'll go and watch a movie," Jake said.

"Where are you going to do that?"

"Over there behind the arcade," he said. I looked and saw a group of students pulling away a black curtain and saw flashing light behind it.

"Care to join me?" he asked.

"Perhaps another time, I'm going to go swimming," I said. There was a small pond where I lived and I loved to go swimming there in the summer.

"Funny, I would have thought someone with fire like you wouldn't like water," Jake teased. I looked at him and sent a small whip of air at his face so it felt like a tiny slap. He jumped back in shock.

"How did you do that?" he asked.

"Air magic," I said cheekily and turned towards the pool leaving him stunned. I found the locker room which, just like the gym locker rooms, had an outfit for me to change into. It was a one piece swimsuit that I decided to make black. I got changed, grabbed a towel and a pair of swim goggles and went into the pool to swim.

The water had a refreshing coolness to it, but it was warm enough that it didn't feel cold as I stepped in. I swam off away from everyone into the deeper end. I did some dives to the bottom of the pool into the serene silence that can only be found under water. Above the water there were cries of delight and splashing, video game noises, and sounds from the movie playing. It was nice to relax and just let myself go. I never wanted to come up so I used air magic to make a bubble under the water so I could breathe. I swam for a little while longer but started getting tired. I decided to get out and dried myself off. After changing, I went to find Noah in the arcade.

I found him at one of the games called FireMan. I looked at the scene and saw a little orange circle chomping little fireballs and fire demons. Noah looked up at me then back at the game.

"It's pretty much PacMan but with fire—and when you do this," Noah made a series of movements on the control panel. Suddenly a huge flame shot out of the game straight at Noah. He jumped back just in time.

"A huge flame tries to kill you," he finished.

"What did you do?" I asked.

"Beat one of the fire demons," Noah said.

"Cool."

I walked over to a game next to him; Donkey Komatite.

"Oh, that one is like Donkey Kong, except he throws boulders. Oh and try not to kill your character or else a stone gets chucked at your face. Not a big one, but it still hurts if it hits," Noah said. I stepped back for the machine.

"I think I'm good," I said and quickly walked away. I went over to the drink stand and found Katie there.

"Hey Selene," Katie said holding a blue bubbling drink.

"What's that you got there?" I asked, pointing to the drink.

"This is bubbling blueberry, my favorite drink. Here let me show you," she said and grabbed my arm and pulled me over to different stalactites hanging from a ledge. They were all different colors of the rainbow.

"Ok, what's your favorite flavor?" Katie asked.

"I don't know—what is there?" I asked.

"Well there's strawberry, raspberry, cherry, orange, lemon, green apple, lime, mint, blueberry, blue raspberry, grape, black licorices, vanilla, cotton candy, and mystery," Katie said smiling. I looked at her, feeling a little overwhelmed with all of the choices.

"Lemon," I said. It was the only flavor I had ever had, but that was in a candy.

"Great," She said and took a glass off the shelf. Then she walked up to the yellow stalactite and broke the tip off. She dropped the rock into the glass. The tip of the stalactite instantly grew back.

"Now do you want it bubbly, fizzy, poppy, or plain?" Katie asked?

"Um, poppy," I shrugged. Katie went over to a nearby ledge with different small waterfalls coming out of the holes in the wall. She placed my glass under one of them. When it was filled she turned to me and said,

"For the final touch," and placed it in a machine that closed it off and shook it like crazy. When it was finished, the yellow rock turned into a yellow drink smelling of lemon. Katie handed me the drink. I took a sip and lemon flavor flooded my mouth.

Then it was like little explosions going off my mouth then it was done.

"That was amazing!" I exclaimed.

"I know, right?" she giggled.

We had finished off our drinks when I saw Jake leave the theater. I walked over to him just as he reached the door.

"Hey, where are you going?" I asked.

"The movie is over and it's getting late," he said.

"Really? What time is it?" I asked.

"Past midnight," he said tiredly.

"Well I guess I should head off to bed too," I said. I left the room and the door closed silently behind us. We walked back together side by side down the hallway heading back to our dorms.

Chapter 21

I awoke to a clamor outside in the common room. I leaped out of bed, grabbed my staff from my bed side and opened the door to a drunken Irene crashing on the couch. I put my staff down and shook my head. I heard Irene moan and went to check on her. She was still in her clothes from yesterday and laying face down on the couch half asleep. I decided to sit her up, I had heard from other people in the Dining Hall and in healing class that this was what you were supposed to do when people were drunk. I made sure her head was leaning forward and went to make a potion from one of my mother's books.

I found all the herbs that I needed in my personal supply that I had brought from home and ground them up to a fine powder. Irene let out a moan again and fell to her side. I stopped what I was doing and repositioned her, then went back to making the potion. After boiling it all till it turned into a purple mush, I took a spoon full of it and brought it to Irene's lips. She sipped at it half consciously, her eyes closed, head sagging. It looked like she had almost no strength or that all of her energy was being used to eat what she was being fed. I fed her spoon after spoon full of the potion until half the mixture was gone. I left Irene to recover a bit—the book had said it would take about ten minutes. I filled some empty bottles with the rest of the potion. By the time I was done, ten minutes had gone by and Irene started waking up. She let out a yawn and blearily opened her eyes.

"Mmmm," she said, *"Wa apped? Were amay?"* I looked at her, confused. She shook her head a little and repeated.

"What happened, where am I?"

"Well, all I know is you woke me up crashing into our dorm completely drunk and were mostly unconscious lying on the couch. I got you into a proper position so that you wouldn't accidentally kill yourself and then proceeded to make one of my mother's potions that helps to shorten the drunk effect and lessens the hangover," I told her. "How are you feeling?"

"Better now. I don't remember much from last night. We stayed at the club until it closed then one of the guys said he was having a party and we all went. I drank way too much. I know that for sure. I remember dancing and then only a few snippets after that," she said.

"Well you should get some rest," I said. She nodded and stood. She wavered for a second then fell back onto the couch.

"I'll help," I sighed, grabbing her arm. I pulled her off the couch and when I had her weight, I helped her to her room. She sat on her bed and then laid down. I pulled the covers over her and she fell fast asleep. I closed the door quietly until it was only open a small crack and went back to my room. The morning sun was shining through the window. I looked at the time and headed off to breakfast.

Jake and Sarah were there already. I sat down with them. Sarah looked tired and Jake looked just as tired as she was.

"Where have you been?" Sarah asked grumpily.

"Asleep and then dealing with a drunk Irene," I replied.

"Figures, she's always partying it up and then getting so drunk that she's sick," Jake said.

"Sounds like you've been to one of these parties," I questioned him.

"Yeah, well um," Jake stuttered.

"Irene used to be his girlfriend," Sarah blurted out.

"Wait what?" I exclaimed. "You never told me," I stared angrily at Jake.

"I didn't see the need to," he said sheepishly.

"She's my roommate, Jake. I should've known," I said and sighed.

"I'm sorry. I should have told you," he said.

"Whatever," I mumbled. I couldn't believe that Jake had dated Irene. I mean it did kind of make sense. She's pretty and Jake's really hot. I started blushing. Jake looked at me and I started blushing more.

Oh no—do I have a crush on Jake? No, that's ridiculous. We are just good friends. Great. Now I'm talking to myself.

"Selene," Sarah called out.

"I'm fine!" I exclaimed, "Just got something on my mind is all."

"Well the bell rang and I was wondering if you guys wanted to do something fun today." Sarah asked.

"Sorry Sarah, I have plans. Also I want to keep an eye on Irene. She wasn't looking too good this morning," I said.

"Fine, Jake how about you?" Sarah asked.

"Maybe another time. I want to see if Irene is okay too. She was a terrible girlfriend but she still deserves to be treated like a person," Jake said. I was surprised and impressed. But I suspected that Jake also wanted to see the dragon egg again.

"Fine. You two go have fun. I'm going to go and wake up Noah. I can't believe he went to the Cavern without me last night," Sarah said and stormed off.

I grabbed some food from the snack bar and loaded my bag up. Jake followed me into the elevator and up to my dorm. I left the food at the table and checked on Irene. She was still deeply asleep but I was going to have to wake her up again to give her more of the potion. I had about an hour until then though. I went into my room where Jake was already seated at my desk. I grabbed the egg and opened the dragon door. I walked inside and Jake followed me. Everything was as we had left it. I walked over to the fireplace and picked out a long metal rod with a wide spoon-like dip in the middle that was on the stand next to the fireplace. I placed the rod over the fire attaching both ends into ledges that had been made just for this. I placed the egg gently onto the spoon part of the rod and stepped back.

"So what do we do now?" Jake asked.

"This," I said and shot more fire into the fireplace. It roared up until it was just below the egg. Then gently, as if you were pulling the cover over a sleeping child, the fire surrounded the egg. The flames receded but the fire around the egg remained.

"Wow, so that's it?" Jake asked.

"Yep, that's it for the next 13 hours," I said.

"So you're going to have to stop this at 10 o'clock on the dot since we started at 9 this morning?" Jake questioned.

"Yeah, I'll just stay up a little later. In the meantime I'm going to find a way to do the tapping while I'm in classes," I said.

"Good idea," Jake said. I walked to the door and Jake followed, taking the cue that it was time to leave.

"I'm going to check on Irene," Jake said.

"Ok. I'm just going to camouflage the door then I'll be right out and join you," I said. I did the spell and watched as the door disappear. Once I was sure it had taken effect I went to find Jake.

Jake was in Irene's room sitting at her desk just watching her.

"How is she?" I asked.

"Not great but she's never been this drunk. Whatever you gave her is definitely working," Jake said.

"Yeah, speaking of which, can you help me? I have to give Irene another dose of the potion," I said.

"Yes, of course," Jake agreed. We walked over to the kitchen area and I grabbed the potion bottle. I added a few drops into a bowl and handed it to Jake.

"Can you fill that up halfway with water?" I asked.

"On it," he said. I concentrated on the rest of the mixture and heated it up in my hand.

"Ok what next?" he asked.

"Stir it until it turns purple," I told him. He did and it was soon purple.

"Follow me," I said. I walked back into Irene's room and went up to her bed.

"Place the bowl under her nose," I told Jake.

"Okay," Jake said unsure. Once the bowl was under her nose, I poured the vial of liquid that was warming in my hand into the bowl. Purple steam shot out as soon as the hot liquid hit the cold liquid in the bowl. The vapors went up into Irene's nose and mouth. Once all the vapors were gone, I removed the bowl and put it back in the kitchen and brought the empty vial back to my room. Jake stayed by Irene's side. I came back and sat down on the bed and looked up at Jake. I took a deep breath and asked him

"Do you still have feelings for Irene?"

"Not really. She was a terrible girlfriend, a real gold digger, even though her parents had just as much money as I had. I eventually broke up with her after I heard her say she was just using me. I still like her but just as a friend. I've never told her before though. We just sort of avoided each other. Besides I have someone else in my mind that is way better than her," Jake looked up at me. I blushed and looked away.

"She'll be waking up soon. We should get out of here before she does," I said and left the room. Jake reluctantly got up and followed me.

"Thank you for helping me today Jake, but I'm going to go and lie down. This morning took a lot out of me. You should go hang out with Sarah—she looked lonely. I'll see you at lunch," I said and half pushed him out the door. When he was out I closed the door and put my back to it. I slid down the door and landed in a heap on the floor.

"What is wrong with me?" I muttered, angry at myself. I knew what it was—I liked Jake, no I think I love him, but I don't want to hurt him. Everyone I have ever loved has gotten hurt by me or by being around me. I care too much for him to see him get hurt, so I have to push him away. My head started to hurt again, so I got up, went into my room and fell asleep on my bed.

Chapter 22

Irene

I woke up and my head didn't hurt like it normally did after getting drunk. I mean it still hurt, but not as much as it normally does. I slowly sat up. I was surprised my body didn't hurt that much either. Then I remembered Selene's potion. I got up and went to Selene's door to thank her. Whatever she gave me really helped. I quietly knocked, but there was no answer.

"She must be out and about," I thought. Good for her, she needed to spend more time out of her room. I found some food on the counter and sat on the couch to eat it. I was starving, but that always happened after I got drunk.

Once I finished eating I went back into my room and grabbed my phone. I saw a lot of missed texts and calls. I quickly read the texts from my friend Sam. The farther I got the more panicked I became. Then I got to the last few texts and screamed. I fell to the floor and cried just wanting to die.

Selene

A scream woke me from my sleep. I shot out of bed and ran to Irene's room, for that was where the scream had come from, and knocked frantically on the door. Irene came to the door after a minute, tears streaming down her face. She pulled me into a hug and cried even more.

"Irene, what's wrong?" I asked worriedly. Irene tried stifling her tears, but couldn't manage to get it out. I got her into a shoulder hug and brought her over to the couch. We sat down and I took both of Irene's hands into my own. I made her look into my eyes and I asked again

"Irene, what is wrong?"

"My-my f-fr-friend S-S-Sam just te-texted me, m-most of it was dr-drunk texts, b-b-but at th-the end she said that M-M-Margaret died last night from al-alcohol poisoning," Irene said through tears and then started crying harder.

"Oh Irene, I'm so sorry," I said. I tried to remember Margaret from our brief encounter, but all I could remember was that she was the nicest of the group and that she had three drinks before I had left. I held Irene as she cried. I let her know that I was there for her while she was grieving.

"Irene, I could make all of this pain go away, but I won't if you don't want to?" I asked her softly.

"You can? How?" she asked desperately looking up at me.

"After my parents died I was just like you. Eventually I found a way to cope with it. Just imagine what is upsetting you—it's okay to cry during this time. Then imagine it slowly evaporating like dew on a blade of grass in the morning sun. Imagine it just lifting away your thoughts, your feelings and out of your life. You will always remember what has happened, but the feeling associated with it will no longer exist in you," I told her softly. I looked at Irene as she closed her eyes. She cried a little harder and as she got to letting it go, Irene just kept crying and crying.

"I can't. I can't let go," Irene cried.

"Would you like my help?" I offered.

"Yeah," she whined and closed her eyes again. This time I placed my hands on Irene's head and imagined with her. I imagined Margaret, cold and dead from the alcohol that had consumed her. Irene let out a cry.

"Let it flow away from you," I spoke quietly. I imagined with Irene to see the image in my mind slowly rise up bit by bit and away until only Margaret's face remained. Then it too slowly dissolved. A light grew from behind the cloud that was Margaret. It rose like the sun bringing it's light. Slowly Irene let go and the cloud faded into the air, so all that was left was the bright glowing light.

"This is what you will think of when Margaret comes to mind," I whispered in Irene's ear. Slowly my eyes opened and saw Irene smiling with eyes closed, still seeing the bright light that is now Margaret.

"Open your eyes. It is time to return to the world around you," I told Irene. I had once stayed like that for days, because I didn't want to return to the world around me. Irene was strong though and slowly opened her eyes. One last silent tear rolled down her cheek and fell to the floor. She sat up and looked at me.

"Thank you," she whispered, "I'm going to go spend a little time in my room."

"Go ahead," I said and watched as she entered her room and closed the door.

Lunch time came and I left Irene in her room to overcome what had happened. Forgetting like that can take a lot out of a person. I used to sleep for a couple hours afterwards.

I walked down to the dining hall still in a little bit of a daze. I grabbed a plate and sat down, watching the food appear on the plate. Sarah and Noah arrived and sat down. They talked for a while, but I didn't listen. Jake came and sat by my side. He said something, but I wasn't paying attention. I was lost in my thought, thinking about how Irene's loss connected so much to my own. They swirled in my mind and my head hurt from the effect. I felt the fire rise in me and I tried to stop it, but I couldn't, so instead I said quietly,

"Jake, get me out of here." He looked at me, but one look was all that took for him to understand. He picked me up into his arms and took me away to an empty classroom. Noah and Sarah followed us, concern flashing across their faces. As soon as the door closed and Jake set me down in the center of the room, my fire came out and surrounded me. Fire was all I could see and it was all I wanted. A door opened and closed, but I was too far away from the world to care. Everything around me grew hotter and hotter. Then there was only fire all around me. No classroom, no people.

"Selene," I heard a voice whisper, "I miss being with you." I snapped out of my trance and saw only fire around me. The fire inside me had been unleashed. I was now inside a fire tornado that I had caused. Quickly I took control. The fire shrank every second and was soon just a small swirling vortex in my hand that I brought back in. Jake was crouched in the corner. Noah was huddled next to him. Sarah had disappeared. I walked up to Jake and touched his shoulder.

"Thank you," I said.

"You can thank me by telling me why this happens. I thought you had this under control," he said a little angrily, as he stood up. Then he took my hand in his and squeezed it lightly.

"Yeah, when you said you had problems with fire I didn't expect it to be this," Noah said.

"Irene's friend Margaret died today. I was helping her to overcome the pain of her loss and got lost in my own, that's all," I told them, "I'm surprised I got this far without losing it. Where did Sarah go?"

"You startled her with this and she ran out the door," Noah said.

"I'm just glad this didn't happen at lunch," Jake said.

"Yeah, speaking of which we should head back. I'm starving," I said. We left but inside I couldn't help but think about the voice.

Chapter 23

The rest of the day went on uneventfully. I found a spell in the dragon book that made the rhythms that the dragon needed for it to hatch and read through the instructions. When 10 o'clock came around I moved the egg off the fires and onto the bed. I then did the spell and the tapping began. It was a nice soft tapping, like someone lightly knocking on a door. Satisfied with my work, I went back into my room and went to bed.

The morning came and I got ready for the day of classes ahead of me. I didn't want to leave the egg but I had too. I double checked that the tapping continued—it still had another day and a half to go. I hid the door once again and walked into the common room. Irene was on the couch in her pjs and a bathrobe.

"Are you ok?" I asked her.

"I'm fine. I'm just taking the day off to clear my head," she smiled weakly. "Thank you for that thing that you did. It really helped me. Before, all I could think of was what Margaret wouldn't be able to do. Now though, I think of all the good times we had."

"You're welcome Irene. Now I have classes to get to," I told her and left.

In intro to air, we learned to make shapes out of air. It was fairly easy. I made a few lazy spirals before we started playing H.O.R.S.E. again. In physical combat we continued to work with our staffs. We are going to be doing this until Friday then we are going to move on to swords. Another tournament would be held in two weeks. I was excited for our next unit though. I had never used a sword. Once class was over I went to fire class.

I walked in and Mrs. Mitchell looked sternly at me.

"Sit down," she said harshly.

I did as I was told.

"I heard from another teacher that you lost control again," she said. I looked at her shocked. Who had seen me? I relaxed after the initial shock though and sheepishly said, "Yeah I did."

"What happened this time?" she asked a little nicer and sat down next to me.

"My roommate's friend died yesterday," I said.

"Ah yes, Margaret Morris. She had great potential as a water mage I heard. Too bad," she said, "But Margaret wasn't your friend, so why did this bother you?"

"Irene was really upset and I wanted to help her, so I did this thing that I used to get over my parents' deaths," I said.

"And what was that?" Mrs. Mitchell asked curiously.

"You close your eyes and imagine what is bothering you, then see it dissolve into tiny pieces. As you do this you'll see a bright warm light come out from behind this cloud of memories—if you did it right that is. Then you imagine the pieces slowly evaporating away, like dew on a blade of grass when the sun rises. Then all that's left is the warm and bright feeling from the light," I told her.

"That sounds like a mental magic spell," Mrs. Mitchell said. "Was Irene able to do it?"

"No, not at first. I had to help her," I said.

"I think you might have some abilities as a mental mage. You should be tested," she said.

"Not right now, maybe later in the year. Right now I just want to learn the classes that I have now. I already have enough trouble with fire," I told her.

"Ok, I understand. But it can be dangerous to not be a trained mentalist. You may accidentally hurt people. Also you're getting better with your fire," she said.

"If what I did was mental magic then I've been a mentalist since I was 6. And thank you for the compliment," I told her.

"Just out of curiosity, this won't make Irene like you would it?" she asked.

"No, that was entirely my fault. I chose to not feel any emotion after the event. That's what caused it," I said.

"Why did you do that?" she asked.

"I was angry before they died. Something in me blamed that feeling and kept it locked up so it wouldn't happen again," I told her.

"I understand, but we are human and we need to feel," she said.

"I know."

"Tell you what—we'll work on fire for the rest of class and your only homework is to feel some emotion," she said.

"Ok, I'll try, but I can't guarantee anything. It's been a long time," I said.

"Alright. Now let's work on conjuring fire again," Mrs. Mitchell said.

Class finished and I decided to skip lunch and check on Irene. She looked exactly as she had this morning.

"Are you alright?" I asked setting my bag down.

"I don't know. I feel like I should be sad about Margaret, but I can only be happy when I think of her," she said.

"That's what we did. The light evaporated all of your sadness toward Margaret's death. This just leaves your memories of her, which I assume are happy ones," I told Irene.

"I know. It just doesn't feel right," she said. I went and sat down next to her.

"If you want, I can try and lessen it so you feel some sadness but it won't overwhelm you" I told her unsure if I could actually do it.

"Could you please try?" she asked.

"Ok." I had her turn away from me and I placed my hands on the sides of her head.

"Imagine Margaret for me please?" I asked. Then I closed my eyes and saw what Irene was imagining, Margaret and Irene playing as children.

"Imagine her dead," I said. The image turned to Margaret dead in a coffin. I saw the light behind the image.

"Now relax," I said. Irene relaxed and I held the image in her mind. Then slowly I took the image apart bit by bit. When it was completely gone, only the light remained. I reached out a hand mentally and grabbed the light. I squished it in between my fingers and it broke apart. Instead of it looking like the sun, the light resembled little stars. Still bright but not as bright as before. I replaced the image of Margaret in the coffin. Then I removed myself from Irene's mind and removed my hands while opening my eyes. Irene turned and looked at me.

"I'm sad about Margaret's death," she said happily and a tear ran down her check. She hugged me.

"Thank you," she sighed.

"You're welcome Irene. Well, you may be taking the day off but I have to get back to class," I told her. She let me go and I stood up. I grabbed my bag and an apple from the snacks I had brought yesterday and headed out the door.

Chapter 24

I met up with Jake in intro to water.

"Where were you at lunch?" he asked.

"I went to check on Irene," I told him.

"We missed you," he said. Same as in air class, we learned how to make shapes out of water. Once everyone got it we played games. It was actually a little fun and I almost felt happy.

I met up with Sarah in potion making and we made some element booster potions. A person who has a low affinity for an element, say for example with water, could drink a water booster potion to improve their affinity for a certain amount of time. How much and for how long depended on the way the potion was made and how much magic was done afterwards. The best potions could even make a non-mage able to have an average affinity with an element. I was fascinated.

We each were allowed to make four—one for each element. Sarah made some average quality and since I had mixed potions before, I made high quality potions. I decided I would give these to Alice over the winter holiday. She always wanted to do magic ever since she saw me do it. I tried to teach her but she had no magic since she came from a non-mage family. I had time left over in class so I read ahead in the recipe book and made 2 vials of spiritual boosters and 2 vials of mental boosters just in case of an emergency. The class ended and I tucked the potions in my bag and went to earth class.

Today's class was inside, which was unusual, since for all the previous week we were outside. I sat down at a desk next to Jake.

"Today as you may have noticed we are inside," Mrs. Blackwood said, "This is for one simple reason—we are not working with natural earth. Yes, I see that you are all confused. Let me explain. The natural earth is what we find outside. Unnatural earth is manmade or hard-to-use elements. Some examples are metals, pottery, and any other materials that use the natural earth. So today we are going to learn how to move and control metal." I was interested in how this would turn out.

"Now please, don't make any weapons or anything inappropriate," Mrs. Blackwood, "I'll pass out these metal bars and what I want you to do is make it a liquid and then make something from it. It's okay if you can't." I was handed a silver looking bar about an inch and a half wide and 6 inches long. I looked at the metal and thought of it as just a pool of melted silver. The bar slowly changed from a solid to a liquid puddle on my desk. I then thought of things to make.

I could do another sculpture or some symbols, but I decided to make my dragon's mark. I formed the head and body and then added a tail and legs. Finally I added wings and claws. I sneaked a peek at my hand, which was still covered with a glove, and added in any details that were missing. When I was done, it was an exact replica of my mark. I then formed a chain and clasp, added a loop to the top of the piece, and made it into a necklace. I looked over at Jake who was struggling after his fifth attempt at trying to make his puddle back into something.

"Wow," he said looking at me and then whispered, "it looks just like your mark."

"That's what I was trying to do," I whispered back to him and placed the necklace over my head and around my neck. I turned to Jake.

"Need some help?" I asked.

"Yes," he said.

"Ok—what do you want to make?" I asked.

"I want to make a pin of the moon," he said.

"Ok then, close your eyes and visualize what you want to make, then see it being made from just your puddle. See it rising up and forming your pin," I told him. He did as I said. Soon his puddle started to rise up and form into the pin shape he wanted. Then he solidified it and it fell to the desk with a soft clang. Jake opened his eyes and saw the beauty of the pin for the first time. It was the silver metal in the shape of a crescent moon with roses winding around it.

"Thank you," he said and then handed me the pin.

"A gift," he said and I took the pin.

"Do you mind if I make one alteration?" I asked.

"Not at all," he answered. I focused on the pin and made the roses red and the stems green.

"You always amaze me," Jake said, "How did you do it?"

I changed the metal to a different color. It's a rule of magic—you can transform an object into something like itself," I told him. Mrs. Blackwood came around to see how her students were doing and to pick up the leftover metal that we had.

"Wow, great job Selene," she said when she saw the pin.

"Actually Jake made the pin," I said, "I made this." I showed her the necklace.

"Where did you see this symbol?" she asked.

"In an old book in the library," I lied.

"Hmm...well you did a good job of remembering its likeness," she said and walked away to check on other students. I tucked the necklace under my shirt and put the pin on.

The bell rang and I went off to spell casting. I wasn't sure what to practice this time. I was well acquainted with water, air, and earth, so I didn't feel the need to practice those. Fire was still too dangerous for me to practice so that was out. I decided to go and visit the library. Mr. Brown signed a pass for me and I left.

I opened the doors to the beautiful library, still overwhelmed by the sight.

"Do you have a pass?" the librarian asked dryly.

"Um...yes," I said quickly and handed her my pass. She signed it and said, "The map of the library is at the center table, if you damage any books you will be responsible for replacing them or paying a fee. Thank you for coming," she said just as dryly as before. She probably said this to everyone that came in.

I walked over to the center table and saw the map pressed under glass on the surface of the table. I found the section for Mage history and decided to go there. There was a lot that I didn't know about the mage world. I got to the section and found a book about the mage war and started reading.

The bell rang just as I was finishing my third book. I left the library and went to check on my dragon hatching.

Chapter 25

Walking into my dorm, I found Irene, Sam, Lauren, and Julia all sitting together on the couch. This had to be about Margaret. Irene looked up at me.

"We've been thinking and since none of them can get out of their grief, we were wondering if you could help them like you helped me?" She asked.

"We'd go and ask one of the other mentalists at this school, but Irene highly recommended you," Julia said.

"Well I guess I could, but I'm not a mentalist," I said.

"Um...Ok," Julia said confused. I started with Sam and worked my way down the couch. By the end, they all felt better and I knew a little more about each of them.

"I just wish we could have said goodbye," Sam said. That gave me an idea.

"Give me some time and maybe I can help with that," I said and left for Jake's dorm.

I got to the door and knocked. A guy that I had never met came out.

"And how may I help you?" he asked with a playful grin. He was obviously flirting with me. I rolled my eyes at his silly antics.

"I would like to speak with Jake please," I said.

"Jake—there's a chick at the door for you," he shouted into the room and then left with a smirk on his face. Once he turned his back I did a little gag. Jake ran up in shock.

"Hey Selene, what's up?" he asked, trying to look cool after being flustered about my being there.

"Do you know where Sarah's dorm is?" I asked him.

"Um...yeah," he said confused.

"Good—take me there," I asked. Jake walked out and closed the door behind him. He started walking down the hall and I took that as a cue to follow him.

"By the way, sorry for Mike. He can be a bit much at times," Jake apologized.

"It's ok. I've seen worse at this school," I told him.

"Hey—you're still wearing my pin," he said. I looked down at the pin and smiled up at him.

"Of course! I don't get many gifts, so I will always cherish it," I said. He smiled and we continued walking.

Soon we reached a door and Jake stopped and knocked. Sarah opened the door and was surprised to see us.

"What are you guys doing here?" she asked.

"Ask Selene," he said.

"I needed to talk to you," I said.

"Come in," Sarah said and we entered. Sarah's dorm looked just like mine but pink everywhere with light colored flooring. We sat on one of the pink couches.

"My roommate is out right now—so what's up?" Sarah asked.

"Well you might have heard that my roommate's friend recently died," I said.

"Yeah I heard about a student dying," Sarah said.

"I was wondering—and I don't even know if you can do this—but could you allow Irene and her friends to talk with Margaret's spirit?" I asked.

"You want me to do what?!" Sarah asked, almost yelling.

"I know, I know, it's a long stretch and I wasn't even sure if you could do it or not, but I figured that a spiritual mage like yourself would have the best chance," I said.

"I don't know if I can even do that," she said, "I mean I've only just learned how to see souls."

"I may have a spell that can do this, but it requires a spiritual mage. Please Sarah, this could give those girls some closure—more than I can give them with my emotion erasing thing," I said.

"Ok. I'll take a look at it but you are going to have to explain this emotion eraser thing," Sarah said and we left her dorm. I explained what I did to Irene and her friends on the way back to my dorm.

We walked in and the girls were still sitting on the couch. I walked past them and into my room. Sarah followed and Jake was about to when Irene called out, "Jake is that you? What are you doing here?"

Jake looked at me and tried to get into my room, but Irene grabbed him and started yelling at him. I looked at him with pity and closed my door.

Sarah was sitting at my window looking out at the sunset. I went and found the book and showed the spell to Sarah.

"I don't know, this looks really tricky," she said.

"Maybe there is something more I can help with," I said and went into my bag to retrieve a vial filled with a glowing liquid.

"Is that a spiritual magic booster potion?" Sarah asked.

"Yeah, I thought it might help," I said.

"That might just do it. But if I start to use too much power, promise me you'll pull me out," Sarah said.

"I promise," I said and handed her the vial. Nervously she drank it and then let out a gasp.

"I can feel the power racing through my veins," she said.

"Good! Now here's the spell book. You should probably do it quickly," I said, handing her the book.

Sarah took hold of it and started the spell. She chanted out the words getting louder and louder as she went. Then a bright white light surrounded her. It grew so bright that I couldn't see her anymore. Then the chants ended suddenly and the light vanished. What was left was Sarah and the spell book sprawled on the ground and Margaret in a semi-transparent state. I ran over to Sarah and saw that she was still breathing. I let her be and turned my attention to Margaret's spirit.

Chapter 26

MARGARET

Darkness was all around me, then a small light appeared far away in the distance. It was my only comfort. As I looked around I became aware of rows of dimmer looking lights herding towards the smaller light. One of the lights pushed past me. I realized they were people.

"Hey watch it will you?" I grumbled. He didn't answer and just kept walking.

"Where am I?" I thought. I looked down at myself and saw the same light around me as the figures around me. I started to panic. So many thoughts raced through my mind and came to one conclusion. I sank to the ground at the realization.

"I must be dead," I thought. "Nooo, I'm too pretty to be dead," I cried.

I finally got myself together and did the only thing I could think of and followed everyone else. It had worked out well for me in life so it might work in death. I started walking with no clue of what to expect.

I walked for what felt like forever but I wasn't tired. The light wasn't any closer and I was becoming content with my new world. Suddenly a new light formed next to me and I stopped my walk to watch. Soon a girl appeared. She looked familiar and I remembered that she was in my spell casting class. Before I could do anything , she grabbed my hand and everything around me fell away. I closed my eyes to shut out the dizzy feeling I was getting. It soon stopped and I opened my eyes to Selene staring at me and that girl who had grabbed me lying on the floor.

SELENE

Margaret stared at me and asked "Where am I?"

"You're in my dorm room," I said.

"Why?" she asked.

"This may be hard to hear but you died yesterday," I said.

"So it is true," she said solemnly and sank to the floor. After a minute she asked, "Why am I here?"

"Your friends are outside in the common room. They wanted to say a proper goodbye to you," I told her.

"They're here?!" she asked, getting a little more excited. She even got off the ground.

"Yes, I'll bring you to them," I said. I walked out into the main room closing the door behind me and saw Irene almost strangling Jake. I knew I wasn't physically strong enough to pull her away so I created a bubble of air between them that pushed them apart.

"Now before you go trying to kill each other again, Margaret would like to speak to all of you," I told them.

"That's a nasty trick to play on us. How can she talk to us when she's dead?" Sam said.

"No—it's the truth," I said and opened the door to my dorm. Margaret floated out. I quickly closed the door so that Jake wouldn't see the unconscious Sarah.

"Margaret," Irene said, not believing her eyes.

"It's me," she said and smiled. I grabbed Jake's arm and pulled him into my room. I wanted to give the friends some time to themselves and also save Jake from another strangling.

"Sarah," Jake cried out, "What happened?"

"She's ok—she just needs to rest. She used up a lot of magic to bring Margaret's soul back," I told him. I levitated Sarah off the floor and onto the bed.

"Tuck in," I said and the bed tucked Sarah in.

"How did you do that?" Jake asked. I threw him a well worn book titled *30 Spells to Make Your Life Easier.*

"Oh," he said. I looked Sarah over and Jake came to stand over me.

"Will she be okay?" he asked.

"Well I'm no nurse, but she seems stable. I have a few potions that should help her to regain her strength quicker," I said. Jake brought over my desk chair and sat next to the bed. I got the potions out of my bag and Jake helped me feed them to Sarah. After a minute her eyes fluttered open and she sat up.

"That was a lot," she said.

"Yeah, good thing I gave you that boost," I said and she laughed.

"How are you feeling?"

"Like I got everything sucked out of me and then put back in but in the wrong way," she said, "But other than that, I'm good."

"Why don't you stay over in my room tonight?" I offered.

"If that's okay with you," she said.

"Of course," I said and she fell back to sleep.

"She probably won't be up till morning," I told Jake, "Want to check on the dragon?"

"Yeah," he said. I removed the enchantment and opened the door.

The egg was where I had left it in the safety of the folds in the bed although it had grown to twice its normal size. The tapping echoed faintly around the room.

"Wow—it's so big," Jake said and crouched down to get a better look.

"I'll be taking the day or at least the morning to finish the preparations for the harvest moon tomorrow," I told Jake.

"I'll cover for you in class and bring you some breakfast and maybe some lunch," he said.

"Thanks," I smiled.

"The other day, I wanted to tell you something, but you sort of shut a door on my face," he said.

"Yeah, sorry about that," I told him.

"No, it's fine. I just wanted to say that, well, you're different from everyone I've ever known and I care about you," he said.

"I know you do. I can see it every day. Look I've never had friends or people that really care about me," I said to him hoping he would stop. He didn't.

"Listen I just want to get this off my chest but I really like you Selene. Would you want to go out on a date with me sometime?" he asked nervously.

"I don't know. Listen, I like you too, but," I sighed, "the last time I really liked someone they got killed. I want to wait a little until I can understand myself more and make sure I won't hurt you," I told him, "Once that happens I will let you know and I'll take you up on that offer."

Jake smiled. "It's there whenever you are ready."

"Thanks Jake," I said. I went back into the bedroom and rehid the door.

"You should probably go back to your dorm room," I said.

"Yeah I probably should," he replied.

"I'll walk you out so Irene doesn't try and kill you again," I joked and opened the door to all the girls laughing and talking. Jake followed me out and I closed the door. Everyone looked up at us and watched as I led Jake to the door.

"Have a good night Jake," I said.

"You too," he said and left. I closed the door and turned to go back into my room.

"Hold it there," Irene said. She stood up and walked over to me. She crossed her arms over her chest and frowned.

"Why didn't you tell me you were dating someone?!" she asked. At the end she was squealing with excitement.

"Wait what?" I asked.

"I mean it's so obvious, right ladies?" Irene said.

"Yeah."

"Yep."

"It's so obvious."

"Okay you have it wrong. We're just friends," I told them all. Irene hugged me and replied,

"It's okay you don't have to hide it from us. I like that you are going out with someone. I mean I don't like that it's Jake, but still it's someone," she said.

"Whatever," I said and broke away from her grasp. As I walked towards my room Sam started singing

"Selene and Jake sitting in a tree K-I-S-S-." I got to my door and closed it before I could hear more. Sarah's snores sounded from the bed. I got into my pajamas and made up a bed on the floor with the extra pillows in the closet. I set an alarm to wake me up at six and drifted off to sleep.

Chapter 27

I woke at exactly 6 a.m. bleary-eyed and tired. Sarah was still in my bed. I yawned and went into the bathroom to shower and get dressed. When I walked out a few minutes later, Sarah was just waking up.

"Hey there sleepyhead," I said.

"Morning to you too," she replied, "I guess I better get back to my room."

She got up and had to sit back down.

"Easy—you used up a lot of magic yesterday. Maybe you should take the day off," I offered.

"No, I'm fine," she said and I helped her up. We walked into the main room and saw Julia, Sam, Lauren, and Irene sleeping on the floor or on the couches. Margaret was sitting at the table looking at her friends. I walked Sarah to the door and let her out, then turned back to Margaret.

"How are you?" I asked.

"I'm not sure. On one hand, I'm with my friends. On the other hand, I know it can't last. I can already feel the pull to return back with the dead," She sighed sadly and looked down. I pulled up a chair next to her.

"Do you want to return?" I asked.

"I don't know. That place didn't make sense and I felt hopeless. Here I feel almost alive but deep down I know that I don't belong," she said.

"Maybe you can show me what it's like," I said taking her ghostly hand. She sent me images of her time in death. It was strange.

"Perhaps if you think of your life, your friends, and family it wouldn't be so bad in that place," I said.

"Perhaps," Margaret said unconvinced.

"Listen, I can see if I can find a way to bring you back. Maybe not alive, but here with your friends forever," I said.

"Really? Wait why are you doing this for me?" she asked, looking at me hopefully.

"I can't guarantee anything, but I'm taking the day off today. I'll look into it. I'm doing this because Irene is my friend and I don't want to see her like she was—like I was so long ago," I told her. She looked at me with a new light in her eyes.

"Thank you Selene, I may not have been your friend in life but know you have one in death," she smiled, "I was going to give this to Irene but I want you to have it." She handed me a small mirror. It was an oval shape with an ornate silver frame and it fit in the palm of my hand.

"It's beautiful," I said.

"Yes, it is. It will allow you to speak with me when I am in the land of the dead. It appeared in my pocket when you brought me back. I just had to hold it and knew what it was. I will have to go soon. Use it to contact me. Just touch the surface and think of me," she said and looked off into the distance. "I must depart now," she said and as I watched, Margaret got fainter and fainter until she was no more. I looked at where Margaret was and sighed. I left the chair and went back to my room. I had preparations to make.

Seven o'clock found me in the dragon room with the dragon book in my hand. The tapping stopped and I started the chants. I chanted and chanted reading the spells on the pages. While I chanted the egg shuddered and shook. This was a sign that the dragon was becoming aware. I kept on chanting. I had only made it through the first page and there were a lot more let.

Four hours later, with my voice a little hoarse, I finished the chants. I was tired and hungry but glad. All that was left to do was to wait until the harvest moon on Friday. Only three days left!

I got up and left the egg on its bed then walked back into my room, put the book away, and hid the door. I walked out into the common room and saw that Jake had come by and dropped off some food. I ate it hungrily and sat on the couch. There would be no point in going to what was left of class so I went back into my room. I had a book about what the afterlife and started reading it to find out whatever I could that might help Margaret. When noon came I went to lunch.

Jake and Noah were at the table.

"Where is Sarah?" I asked.

"She felt tired and just wanted to rest today," Noah answered.

"So how did it go?" Jake asked.

I looked at him with daggers.

"How did what go?" Noah asked.

I sighed. "Meet me at my dorm room after classes and I'll show you. You might as well bring Sarah too."

"Sorry," Jake whispered to me.

"Never mind—I can't keep it a secret forever I guess," I whispered back.

"Hey what are you whispering about?" Noah asked and raised his eyebrows.

"Nothing of your concern," I told him. For once Noah was silent. We ate the rest of lunch in peace.

After classes were over Jake, Noah, and a tired Sarah found themselves in my dorm common room.

"So what is this about?" Noah asked.

"Follow me," I replied and led the way to my room. Once everyone was inside I closed and locked the door.

"Did you just lock us in?" Sarah asked.

"No, I locked everyone else out," I explained. I walked over to the hidden door and removed the enchantment.

"Whoa!" Noah said. "I did not see that coming." He walked over and tried to open it. "It's locked," he said.

I removed my glove to unlock the door. Sarah and Noah gasped. I realized this was the first time they had seen the mark.

"Is that a burn?" Sarah asked and almost fainted. I nodded and placed my hand on the doorknob, turning it. The door swung open easily. The egg was where I had left it on the bed. It had grown since the morning and was now the size of a basketball.

"What is this place?" Noah asked.

"This is the dragon room," I said.

"A dragon room—but there hasn't been a dragon in hundreds of years," Sarah said amazed.

"Well there will be one soon," I told them and pointed to the egg. Sarah knelt down next to the egg in astonishment. Noah stood over her looking at the egg.

"How did you get this?" he asked and looked at me.

"Dean Autumn gave it to me. When I went to see her, apparently my ability with fire reminded her of a dragon mother.

She gave it to me to try and hatch it," I said fondly. I went and picked up the egg.

"Can I hold it?" Sarah asked.

"I don't know—let me check," I said and I put the egg back down carefully. I went out into my room and found the dragon book. I came back with it open in hand.

"When the egg is in the final stages of hatching it is important that only the mother or caretaker of the dragon touches or handles the egg. If it is touched by any other it can confuse the baby dragon into thinking its mother is someone else," I read.

"I guess not," Sarah said.

"Maybe when the dragon is born?" I replied.

"When will that be?" she asked.

"Friday night if everything goes as planned," I said.

"Would you like us to be there for you?" Jake asked.

"You know what—that might be nice," I said, "Why don't you all come over and we can have a little party until it gets dark."

"That sounds like fun," Sarah said.

"I will be there," Noah replied. We walked back into my room and I hid the door. A knock came from my bedroom door. I walked over and opened the door wondering who it could be. I opened the door to Irene.

She saw everyone in my room and shyly said, "Thank you for what you did for my friends and I. We greatly appreciate it." Then she left and ran into her room.

"That was weird," Jake said, "I've never seen her be nice to someone, let alone thank someone."

"Really, she's been nice to me since I've known her. Well except when I first met her," I said.

"Yeah she used to be a real jerk to everyone while we dated. I guess she became nicer up after we broke up," Jake said, "Which makes sense since when I broke up with her I kind of told her that she had been acting like a jerk."

"Yeah, that can change a girl," I laughed.

"Hey, it's almost dinner time," Sarah said, "Shall we go? I'm hungry."

"Of course!" I agreed and we all headed to dinner.

Chapter 28

Friday finally came. I woke up in the morning stressed for the events to come. Through all of my classes I was a wreck. I lost control of my air whip and almost hit Mr. Nelson instead of the apple in front of me and I accidentally hit Coach Swift instead of the practice dummy when he came to see how I was doing. It had just been a bad morning. I walked into Mrs. Mitchell's classroom and just groaned.

"Ok, what's up with you?" she asked.

"I can't get anything by you, can I," I said sarcastically.

"No, but you can try all you like," she smiled and sat next to me, "Now, what's really going on here?"

"I'm just a little stressed out," I said vaguely. She raised an eyebrow at me.

"Ok, maybe a lot stressed out."

"Well then today's lesson is perfect. We are going to be meditating. It will help to center you and your fire" she said.

Meditating was nice. I was still stressed after, but not as much as before. I walked into the dining hall for lunch. I saw Jake, Sarah, and Noah sitting at our table. To my surprise I also saw Irene sitting there.

"Why are you sitting here?" I asked.

"Well hello to you too," she replied and took a bite of her food.

"Hello, now why are you sitting here?" I asked again. She swallowed and spoke.

"You are keeping secrets from me," she said, standing up. Then she slammed her hand on the table and looked me straight in the eye, "I want to know what you are hiding. All of your friends know. They hang out in your room, you lock the door on me so I can't get in, and you spend way too much time in there. What are you hiding?"

Everyone at the table looked at me. I guessed that this would happen eventually—just not so soon.

"I'll tell you, but not here. I'll explain everything tonight," I said calmly.

"Fine," she said and picked up her plate and went back to her table. I sat down, put my bag on the table and face planted into it.

"Are you okay?" Noah asked.

"Do I look ok?" I said, my voice muffled by the bag.

"No you don't," Jake said and chuckled.

"Thanks for the compliment," I said sarcastically, still muffled by the bag. I lifted up my head and rolled my eyes.

"I'm just under a lot of stress and Irene isn't helping!" I exclaimed.

"Whoa calm down Selene. Everything will be okay. We'll all be there to support you," Jake said and smiled. I smiled back and did some of the meditation I had learned today. Then I got my plate.

The rest of the school day passed in a blur and by the time spell casting class was over I was nervous again. Katie took notice of this.

"Why do you look so nervous?" she asked.

"I just have something important to do tonight and I don't want to mess it up," I said.

"Well no matter what it is, I think you'll do great. You are one of the best mages I know," Katie said and smiled. Her smile warmed me up inside and eased some of my nervousness.

"Thanks Katie," I replied.

"No problem," she shrugged, "I have to go." And with that she turned down a hallway and I walked past.

I got to my room and Irene was there sitting on one of the couches. She motioned for me to sit. I swallowed hard and sat.

"So, what's going on?" she asked.

"Before I tell you, you have to swear you won't tell anyone else," I told her.

"Fine, now spill," she said.

"I'm hatching a dragon," I said quickly. Irene opened her mouth and shot her finger up as if to say something and then closed her mouth and dropped her finger.

"Wait, what? That was not what I thought you were going to say," she laughed.

"Well what did you think I was going to say?" I asked. Irene started to play with her hair.

"I thought you were having a thing with Jake" she mumbled.

"What?"

"I thought that you and Jake were a couple and were making out in your room and then when Noah and Sarah came in I thought that you were both doing it. I know it sounds wrong, but that's what I thought," she said angrily and then sheepishly. I stared at her and laughed.

"That's what you thought?" I said, still laughing.

"Yeah and I was mad because I thought Jake was with you," she said.

"Irene, if I had a boyfriend I would tell you, but I don't. I don't like those sort of things" I sighed.

"Oh, ok. So what is this dragon hatching you were talking about?" she asked.

I chuckled a little to myself and said, "Follow me."

I led Irene to my room and showed her the egg and the room it was in.

"Amazing! There hasn't been a dragon hatching in hundreds of years. Where did you even get the egg?" she asked.

"Dean Autumn," I told her.

"She gave you her egg?" Irene asked.

"You knew she had one?" I countered.

"I used to come here all the time when I was little. Dean Autumn would let me look at it. I would stare at it for hours imagining what the dragon would look like," she said dreamily.

"So when is it going to hatch?" she asked.

"Tonight as soon as the sun goes down," I said and pointed to my window where the sun was already setting.

"So we don't have much time," she said.

"No we don't, but everyone is coming over to help me in any way they can. You can help if you want," I said.

"Of course I'll help," she said. I smiled and started to prepare the room for tonight.

Chapter 29

The room was prepared and there were snacks that everyone had brought from either the dining hall snack bar or from their personal stashes they had brought from home. Sarah had elected herself to go and get dinner for everyone later. As the last rays of sunlight filtered through the window outside I let out a sigh and turned to everyone.

"Thank you all for being here to help me through this. I couldn't ask for better friends," I said. I went and sat on the dragon bed where the egg was. I removed my hand from my glove and those who hadn't seen the mark yet gasped. I ignored them and scooped up the egg into my arms and placed it in my lap.

The last rays of sunlight filtered in through the window and then faded completely. The egg began to make a pecking sound. It was the dragon trying to hatch. Quickly I drew on my fire and heated up my hands to the hottest temperature I could muster hoping it was enough. It wasn't going to be easy. I had to keep it constantly going without losing control. Every time I renewed the heat in my hands a new emotion came at me with a memory to coincide, causing me to lose control for a moment. I had to close my eyes after a couple hours to help fight the oncoming emotions and memories. I heard Sarah leave and come back with food. Jake offered me some food but I couldn't even answer him through the onslaught of memories and emotions. Everyone was doing their best to support me.

Around 1:00 a.m. a memory hit me so hard I started crying and lost control for a few seconds. I felt a hand on my shoulder and heard murmurs of them encouraging me, but I couldn't hear what they were saying. My whole body was sweating from the heat I was creating as I assumed everyone was too. I was in full concentration trying to keep the control I was slowly losing.

By 4:00 a.m. I was finally starting to lose the battle to control my emotions. I opened my eyes to see if I could get help from anyone. Everyone was asleep, except for Jake, who was sitting in the corner watching me.

"Jake," I whispered. My voice was hoarse and dry from the amount of energy I was using. He got up and walked over to me. He sat down next to me on the bed and placed his arm on my shoulder. I looked and saw his arm was getting burnt from my touch. I tried to shrug his arm off, but he kept it in place.

"You'll get burnt," I whispered hoarsely.

"Yes, but you need the support," he said. And with that, a flood of energy flowed into me from Jake's hand. I looked at him in shock.

"Use it well—I believe in you," he said and fell back on the bed into a deep dreamless sleep from the energy he just gave to me. His hand fell away and I stared at him in shock, but not for long. I had a job to do. With Jake's energy added to my own I gained better control and closed my eyes again, concentrating.

When light reached my closed eyes through my eyelids, I opened them and saw that the sun had risen and was streaming through the window in my room. I brought my fire back inside and looked at the egg. It was much bigger than it had been and had a few cracks from where the dragon had tried to get out before I sent it back to sleep. Other than that it seemed fine. Now that it was cooling down, the dragon woke up inside the egg and started to break the shell. The sound of cracking could be heard around the room. Sarah woke to the sound first followed by Irene, then Noah. Jake remained asleep. Everyone stared at the egg as the cracks grew bigger. Then with the loudest crack of all, the egg shell shattered and flew everywhere.

All that was left was a little baby dragon the size of a small puppy. It was a beautiful, soft, snowy white dragon with black-tipped scales and horns. The most stunning thing was its bright, brilliant blue eyes—the color of sapphires. As we stared it got up on its legs, wobbling a little, and slowly turned around in a circle. Upon seeing my hand with the mark it decided to lick it. Its tongue was soft yet rough at the same time and tickled. The saliva left behind from the lick was warm but not quite hot. I let it sit in my lap staring at my hand as this was the acceptance time for the dragon. After a minute the dragon bowed its head to my hand and the saliva glowed blue and went into my skin. The burn look of the mark disappeared slowly and looked more like a tattoo. The dragon on my hand looked exactly like the dragon sitting in my lap and now it had a stream of white blue fire streaking out its mouth that coiled around my wrist.

"Hi there little guy," Sarah said gently.

"Incredible," Irene said and turned her head to the side. The dragon mirrored a gesture the same as hers.

"It is definitely a sight to behold," I said and the dragon turned to me and jumped onto my chest.

"Hi master," it said. I stared at it in surprise. The voice was that of a little boy so I assumed that the dragon was male.

"Hi," I said back.

"What would you like to name me?" he asked.

"What do I want to name you?" I repeated to him.

"Uh, Selene, are you talking to the dragon?" Irene asked. Then I realized that he hadn't said any of this out loud. It was all in my head.

"Um...yeah. We are talking through our minds," I said "He wants to know what his name is."

"Well it should be something meaningful," Sarah said.

"Yeah the last dragon was called Peace, because it was to keep peace," Irene said.

"I think I have a name. What about Isaac?' I said.

"Not bad," Noah said, shrugging.

"Why that name?" Sarah asked.

"It's my father's name," I said. Everyone was quiet. They all knew about my parents.

"Are you okay with him being named after your father?" Irene asked.

"Yeah—my father was a good man and a powerful mage. I assume this little guy will become a very good and powerful dragon," I said tickling his stomach, "So Isaac will be his name." I looked the baby dragon in the eyes and spoke through my mind to his and said, "Your name is Isaac."

"I accept this name and will give it the honor it deserves," he thought to me. I smiled.

"He accepted the name," I said.

"Good. Now I'm going to get some proper sleep—in a bed," Irene said.

"Me too," Sarah said.

"Yeah I need to get back to my dorm," Noah said.

"Come on Jake," he said kicking Jake lightly in the leg. Jake didn't stir.

"What's wrong with him?" Sarah asked and kneeled down next to him concerned.

"He gave me his energy to help me through the night," I said.

"So he's just drained, like I was?" Sarah questioned.

"I assume so," I said, "I'll keep an eye on him today."

"If you need any help, let us know," Noah said yawning and they all left.

I closed the door to my room behind them and set Isaac on the ground. He scuttled over to the pool of water and stuck his feet in. He started splashing through the water and rolling around getting the goop of the egg off him. I let out a little laugh and walked into my closet to change realizing I was as slimy as Isaac was. Once I was changed I went over to Jake.

He was still unconscious. His breathing was slow and even, so he must have been regaining the energy that he gave. I placed my hand on his head and gave back what energy I had left. I felt weak but I had felt this way before and shook it off. I went into my room to make the energy renewal potions like the ones I had made for Sarah. I also decided on making a different type of energy potion since I hadn't slept last night and probably wouldn't be sleeping today since I had to look after Isaac. I got out the ingredients and ground them all up, added a little of my energy, and poured it into two vials. Then I made the second potion. I closed off the vials and shook them all. I downed one of the energy renewals and the energy potion.

I brought the other energy renewal potion back into the dragon room. I went to Jake and sat him up on the dragon bed. He let out a groan and I did my best to soothe him by rubbing his shoulder. I tilted his head back slightly and opened his mouth, then poured the contents of the vial into his mouth and made him swallow. After he swallowed all of it, I levitated him up and onto my bed and tucked him in. The levitation had used up the energy I had gained from the potion though. I was still weak and probably wouldn't be able to do magic for the rest of the day. Isaac was done with his little bath and walked wobbly to me. He jumped onto my shoulders where he proceeded to wrap around them, his tail loosely wrapped around my neck, and fell fast asleep. I petted the dragon's back and went to clean up the rooms from the little party we had.

Cleaning took a while and wasn't easy with a sleeping dragon on my shoulders. I finally finished and sat down at the window and looked out into the world. It was a bright and beautiful day. People were practicing on the lawn outside. Balls of fire shot out and water was thrown. It looked like a lot of fun. Isaac let out a snort of hot air on my neck and brought me back to reality. I remembered that I still had to bring Isaac to see Dean Autumn. I didn't want to leave Jake but decidd he would be fine just sleeping. Just in case, I left a note on my desk for him and another energy vial for him to take. I walked out of the dorm with my cloak covering my shoulders to hide the dragon and set off towards Dean Autumn's office.

I reached her office quickly. There were voices coming from within her office so I patiently waited on the other side of the door. That way, when they came out, no one could accuse me of eavesdropping.

Chapter 30

Dean Autumn

"Robert, I'm going to ask you one final time. Who is Selene Woods?" I asked.

"I don't know. That's what I keep telling you. All I know is that she belongs to a family of very powerful mages. I know not which family it is though. Someone put her into this school so her application was accepted and given to me. That was all I was given," Robert replied.

"Well then why did you recruit her if you didn't know who she was?" I asked, almost shouting.

"She was on my list to recruit. There was no name. Just an address and an aging picture," he said softly. I sat down in my chair and massaged my temples.

"Then I want you to find out who wanted her recruited and why. And see if they know who she is!" I yelled at him, "Now leave me." Robert needed no more than that and left. No sooner had he left than there was a knock on the door.

"What now?" I thought.

"Come in," I said politely. Selene came in, hooded in her cloak.

"What is it Selene?" I asked, shocked that she was here, but I hid it with a smile. Did she hear any of what I had been discussing? She didn't say anything—she just took off her cloak. From underneath her hair two blue eyes stared out at me. I stood and walked around the desk and stared in amazement.

"You said to come to you when I had hatched the dragon. So here I am," she said. I looked at her in amazement.

"Do you know what this means?" I said.

"No," she said, concerned.

"We finally have a fighting chance against our enemies," I said.

"Wait what?!" she exclaimed, surprised by my words.

"Five hundred years ago the last dragon was killed. With that we had no champion to fight our enemies. But now we do," I said and looked at her admiringly.

"What enemies? I thought the war ended when our enemies disappeared," she said.

"Well yes and no. They hid the dragon killing weapon from us and never went back into full out war, but Douglas Donahue still lives. He and his followers attack randomly and in packs. This means that they are still fighting us, but there is no full out war, yet," I told her.

"So the war never ended," she said.

"Yes and now, once this little guy gets bigger and stronger, you both will be able to help us in fighting our enemies," I said practically jumping for joy. Selene looked horrified.

"I don't want any part in your war," she said coldly.

"Too bad my dear. Now we must report to the Council of Mages as soon as possible," I said and grabbed her wrist. She ripped it out of my grasp and stared at me.

SELENE

So many thoughts were swirling in my head. I was supposed to fight in a war that had been going on for over five hundred years. This was crazy.

"I'm not going with you," I said.

"Oh but you must. You don't know how long we have waited for a dragon to be born," she cried out.

"I don't care. You're crazy and we aren't going," I shouted. Isaac woke up and started snarling.

"Please come with me. I don't want to have to force you," she said nicely. I stared at her shocked. So this was the terrifying Dean Autumn everyone knew.

"Never," I said just as icily to her and turned to walk out the door.

"Fine then, have it your way," She said and lashed out with a hidden chain concealed in the sleeve of her outfit. She used metal magic to guide it like a snake towards me. I turned at her words and tried maneuvering out of the way, but the chain was too fast and it started twisting around my arms. It twisted so tightly that I let out a cry of pain.

"Now you will come with me," she said and started dragging me across the room. Isaac jumped off my shoulders and ran at her. He was fast but Dean Autumn was faster and grabbed a cage hidden in the shadows of her room, trapping Isaac in it.

"No," I cried out weakly and tried to use magic to free myself, but I was still too drained. With one hand holding Isaac's cage and my chains, she opened a secret door in her office, pulled me in and closed the door.

Chapter 31

Darkness surrounded us. I was scared for the first time since I was six years old. Dean Autumn opened the door again, but it wasn't her office that was on the other side. It was a long hallway leading to huge doors. She pulled me up and pushed me through the doorway and then followed, closing the door behind her. She released Isaac from his cage and he leaped out and jumped onto me. I tried to pet him but the chains just got tighter.

"Are you okay mistress?" he asked me.

"I'll be fine. Just behave and try to hide under my hair and cloak as best you can," I told him.

"Yes, mistress," he replied and hid under my hair, his tail wrapping around my neck again.

"Come along dear," Dean Autumn said and pulled at my chains. I stumbled behind her with each pull. We got closer and closer to the doors at the end of the hall. Once we were right in front of them we stopped.

"I must speak to the Council," Dean Autumn called aloud. At first nothing happened and then the huge doors opened. Once they were fully open she pulled me through them. The place was huge. There were stands on which people were seated facing a central dais with eight chairs around a semi-circular desk. I assumed that these were the council members or the higher members. There was one for each main branch of magic. I was pushed into the middle of the dais and in front of the council. Dean Autumn stood next to me and removed my chains.

"Sorry for the way I had to bring her but she refused to come of her own accord," she said.

"And who is she?" a man in front of us said.

"This is Selene Woods, although her birth name remains hidden to us. She has hatched a dragon and it has bonded to her," she said.

"Where is this dragon now?" The same man said. Dean Autumn looked at me and pulled my hair and cloak away from my shoulders. Isaac could now be seen by all and the whole room gasped.

"So what you say is true Autumn. We have some decisions to make with this new information. Girl how old are you?" The man addressed the last part to me.

"Seventeen and my dragon was just hatched this morning," I said, sensing his next question.

"Hmm....You are no more than a child," he said, "You must have power to be able to pull off this feat."

"That she does," Autumn said.

"Show me," he said.

Autumn leaned over to me and whispered, "Show them your ability with fire or you'll be sorry." So as I digested her threat, I decided to take her advice. I gathered what energy I had left and started to make my fire. It started as a little flame as I was still drained from this morning, but I found some more magic within me and sent it towards the flame which grew to be a huge column of fire. I brought it back in and looked at the council's astonished faces.

"Who are you young lady?" An older woman council member said.

"Selene Woods," I answered.

"No, your family name?" she asked.

"I will not say it."

"Fine, we will find out for ourselves," the man said. And with that, four guards came onto the dais and pushed me to my knees. I tried to fight but I was too weak. Isaac was knocked off my shoulders and was crying out next to me. I was held on my knees facing the council with my hands behind my back. Two guards held my arms and the other two held my shoulders. Slowly one of the people in front of me stood and walked around the desk and stood before me. I kept struggling with my captors as he did so. When he reached me, he grabbed my face and made me look him in the eye.

"I am Mark Crawford—the most powerful living mentalist mage. There is no use struggling. It will only make it worse. I will find out your true name. It is what the Council demands," he said.

He moved his hand and placed it on top of my head. I tried to maneuver out of it but the guards held my head still. I felt him enter my mind and I closed my eyes from the pain. He started searching through all of my memories and the knowledge that was in my head. He got closer and closer into the part of my mind where I hid away my past. His magic touched it and something in me snapped. I screamed as I felt a surge of power fly out of me that I never knew I had. Mark went flying backwards and hit his head hard on the ground. This caused the guards to loosen their grips in shock and I freed myself from them and used that same unknown power flowing through me to push the guards away. They fell back and one of them went flying across the room.

"We're leaving," I said to Isaac and ran towards the doors. He jumped onto my shoulders as I walked away.

"Don't let her escape," someone said from behind me and the doors began to close. I started running as fast as I could and barely made it through the doors. I stopped and watched the doors close behind me with a thud. I ran back to the door that led to Dean Autumn's office and went inside. I closed the door and heard a soft click that I had not heard the first time. I opened the door and I was back in the office. I ran out the door and didn't stop until I got into my dorm where I ran straight into Jake.

Dean Autumn

"What did you bring to us!" Council member Hunter bellowed.

"She hatched a dragon. You told me if that ever happened to bring the one who hatched it in!" I shouted back.

"But she is a strong force, with dangerous qualities. She has almost killed our best mentalist, injured four of our guards, and was able to escape!" he shouted.

"I had no idea that she was this powerful," I said. Mark let out a groan and Hunter walked over. Mark sat up and shook his head.

"What did you find out about her?" Hunter asked him.

"She is very powerful. I was only in the area I needed to be for a second. Then she shut me out before I could get any deeper," Mark sighed.

"So what did you find out?" member Hunter repeated.

"She comes from the Mystic family," he sighed.

I couldn't believe what he said. He tried to stand up and almost fell back down. Hunter grabbed his arm and sat him back down. Then he turned to me.

"You are to leave now and watch out for what this girl does next. No one is to know of this information. I will personally research this further. I have suspicions that she may be working for our enemies," he said.

"The Mystic family died out sir. She can't be one of them," I said.

"I know—so watch her closely. Now go," he said. I half-walked, half-ran out of the room and back into my office. I sat down with a sigh at my desk.

I had no intentions of this happening to her and how could she possibly be a Mystic? They died out over ten years ago and there were no recorded childbirths. I needed to apologize to her, but how? She most likely wouldn't trust me anymore. I got up from my desk and left to go to Selene's dorm.

Chapter 32

SELENE

I looked up at Jake for a moment and then pushed past him into my room.

"Is everything okay?" he asked.

"No, everything's not okay. I'm leaving," I said and started packing up my things. Stuff started floating into my bag as I did a spell.

"Wait—what?! Why?" Jake asked confused. I fell to the floor and for the first time broke down and cried about something other than my parents.

"Whoa—Selene what happened? What did this to you?" Jake asked again and sat down on the floor beside me.

"Dean Autumn told me to go to her office once Isaac was born," I told him through my tears, "And then...and then..." I started crying harder.

"It's okay, it's okay," Jake said and put his arm around me. I fell into his grasp and cried into his chest.

"You don't have to tell me," he said, "But I would like to know what happened to you." I sniffled a little and got control over my emotions.

"She tied me up and caged Isaac. She took us through a secret door in her office and presented us to the council of mages. She told me I was to be their new champion in the war," I said.

"What war?" Jake asked.

"Remember the one you told me about 500 years ago? Well it never ended. It has just been less all-out war and more like small attacks here and there," I told him.

"So what did the council do?" he asked. I started crying hard again. Jake held me tighter and just waited. I eventually got myself together.

"I showed them my ability with fire and then they wanted to know about my family. I refused to tell them and I was restrained. They had a mentalist come and enter my mind trying to find the information. I don't know what happened, but something in me fought back. The mentalist was thrown back and then I directed that energy to the guards and they went flying back. I took my chance and got out of there and ran back here," I said and started crying harder. Jake put his head on mine and just held me tight.

"I'm so sorry you had to go through that," he said.

"I need to leave. I can't stay here," I said quietly.

"I know, but I don't want you to go. I'll miss you too much—which is why I'm coming with you," he said. I looked up at him in surprise.

"You belong here. You need to stay," I said.

"If you're leaving, I'm going with you," he replied stubbornly.

"Then I'll stop you," I said and stood up. He followed my actions.

"You can't stop me," he said and made a motion with his hand. A suitcase appeared in his hand. My bag was packed and I grabbed it. I knew that I could stop him but something in me didn't want to.

"Well let's go then," I said and walked into the common room and left a note for Irene. I opened the door and Dean Autumn was there standing in the hall with her hand raise ready to knock. I dropped my bag and instantly called up an air whip, wrapping it around her.

"Please just listen to me," she said quickly.

"Why should I listen to you?!" I asked aggressively.

"Because I wish to apologize," she said. I didn't loosen her restraints but I listened to what she said next.

"I didn't know that they would do that. I was just following my orders and I am truly sorry for what they did to you. I can't imagine what it must have felt like," she said and then she saw our bags.

"You're leaving," she gasped.

"I can't stay where I'm going to be treated like this," I spat at her.

"You too Mr. Morales?" she asked.

"I don't want Selene to be by herself anymore," he said.

"I technically can't allow you leave," she said and then saw my expression. Nothing was going to stop me from leaving.

"But...but here's what I'll do. You can take the next week off. I'll give you plenty of food for the dragon, but please come back," she pleaded.

"Fine," I said with no intentions of ever coming back. I released her and she handed me a small drawstring bag.

"Here is the dragon food and I'll send a stone to bring you both back. In the bag is a transport stone that will take you home," she said. I pushed past her and walked away to the main doors to leave.

We walked outside and I turned to Jake.

"Where is your car?" I asked.

"Why?" he asked.

"Because I don't trust the stone she gave us, so other than flying, the only way I see to get to my house is driving," I said and threw the stone on the ground and crushed it under my foot.

"Okay. My car is this way," Jake said and we walked to the side of the school where the parking lot was. I spotted Jake's black Mercedes Benz. We got in and Jake turned on the car.

"So where do you live?" he asked.

"Depends on where the school is," I said. He pulled up a map on his phone and pointed to a spot on it. I looked around and surprisingly saw that I lived fairly close to the school. I pointed to a spot a few miles away covered in green.

"I live around here," I said.

"Ok," Jake replied and drove off. I stared out the window the entire way listening to the radio. Isaac was sticking his head out the window while sitting on my lap and sticking his tongue out like a dog. I started seeing some familiar trees and started looking out the front windshield.

"Turn down here," I said when we got to Alice's driveway. Jake pulled up the half-mile long driveway.

"Are you sure it's this way?" Jake asked.

"Yeah, it's just a really long driveway," I said. We soon pulled up to the house and Alice's mom came out.

"Stay here," I thought to Isaac and I got out of the car.

"Selene," Alice's mom called out. She rushed out and gave me a big hug. "We missed you dear."

I hugged her back. She held me at arm's length and noticed Jake.

"And who is this?" she asked in a teasing way.

"This is Jake. He is a friend from school. We have this next week off, so I thought I'd come home and visit you," I said.

"Well I'm glad you did. Why don't you get settled back into your house and come over later for dinner?" she offered.

"Of course," I said and she went back into her house. I went back to the car and got my bag and staff, then hid Isaac underneath my cloak. Jake grabbed his bag and waited for me.

"I hope you don't mind hiking," I said and walked into the woods.

Chapter 33

We reached my treehouse in five minutes. I levitated myself up and opened the door. I dropped my bag in the living room and let it unload itself.

"Selene," I heard Jake call. I went back onto the front porch and saw Jake still on the forest floor.

"Um...I don't know how to fly," he called up. I sighed and levitated him up. He came up and landed unsteadily. Jake walked in and looked around the house.

"Well, I might as well give you a tour," I said and did just that. I showed him the kitchen, dining, and living room. Then I showed him the guest bedroom and connecting bathroom. I technically didn't have plumbing, but it was still a bathroom, just not a modern one. He put down his bag in the bedroom and started unpacking a little. I put Isaac down in my room where he curled up into a ball and fell fast asleep on my pillow. I put my cloak on the hook by the door and went into the living room. I sat on the couch and put my head in my hands. I heard Jake walk in and I looked up.

"Are you okay?" he asked.

"I will be eventually," I said and started to do my emotion release exercise.

"So what do you do for entertainment around here?" Jake asked.

"Well I don't have electricity if you were thinking of video games or something. I normally take forest walks or read. When it's warmer I go swimming in the lake nearby," I said.

"Oh, ok. So what do you want to do?" he asked.

"Well I have a few places to show you before we go to dinner," I said and led him out to the back balcony. I levitated us both down to the forest floor and led Jake past my gardens to my parents' graves. I sat down in front of the markers while Jake remained standing.

"What is this?" Jake asked.

"These are my parents' graves. I wanted you to see them," I said.

"Oh," Jake said and sat next to me.

"I gave my father a stack of rocks and the magic left over in his body created the moss. The same for my mother—I planted some seeds for my mom and they grew into these brilliant flowers," I told him.

"It's beautiful," he said. The moss grew brighter and the flowers straightened up a bit.

"They like you," I said. He smiled. The birds twittered overhead and a breeze blew through the trees.

"I missed this—the quiet and calm," I said.

"It's nice," Jake said. We sat for a few minutes and it was bliss. I looked at the sun and calculated that it was a little after 4 pm.

"We should go get ready for dinner," I said and got up. Jake followed me and I levitated us up to the house.

"Wear something nice. Dinner at their place is really formal," I told him and then went into my room.

I walked out of my room 20 minutes later in a black off-the-shoulder dress with black heels. I put in silver earrings that looked like leaves and tied my hair up into a bun with curled tendrils of my hair framing my face. Jake walked out in a dress shirt and khakis. He had brushed and put gel in his hair and wore dress shoes. He looked me up and down.

"You look great," he said.

"Thank you," I said.

"Is it weird that I feel overdressed?" he asked.

"No it's not. I felt that way my first time but, like I said, Alice's family dress up for their dinners so you won't feel overdressed once we get there," I told him. I levitated us down and let Jake walk while I floated over the ground. It wasn't the easiest thing to walk in the forest with heels on. We reached Alice's house before night had fallen.

"Hey!" Alice cried out when she saw me. She ran up to us and embraced me in a hug. She was wearing a long blue dress that reminded me of the night sky.

"Hey Alice—this is Jake," I said. See looked Jake up and down and leaned over to whisper in my ear

"He's cute! Are you dating him?"

"What? No," I whispered back.

"Hi, I'm Alice," she said to Jake and stuck out her hand.

"So this is the famous Alice," he replied and took her hand shaking it.

"Come in! Mom made your favorite," Alice said and turned to go back inside.

"Ooo, yum," I said and followed her inside. Jake followed me and we entered the kitchen. A delicious aroma filled the air. Alice was right—her mom had made my favorite dinner. I saw Alice's dad in the living room and went over to him.

"Good evening," I said.

"Ah, Selene, what a pleasure to have you over," he said and got up out of his recliner and hugged me.

"It's good to see you too," I told him.

"And who is this young fellow?" he asked, pointing to Jake.

"Don't you remember dear? I told you about Jake and how he's Selene's new friend," Alice's mom called from the kitchen.

"Oh right. It must have slipped my mind," he said.

"Dinner will be done in a few minutes. Why don't you help set the table dears?" Alice's mom asked.

"Of course," I told her and with a little nudge at Jake, we helped set the table with Alice. Once it was set, everyone sat at the table—except Alice's mom who was still cooking.

"So how has school been?" Alice asked.

"Interesting, um...It's just a new experience that I have to get used to," I said.

"I bet its fun there," she sighed.

"But don't you like your school?" Alice's father chimed in.

"I do, but it can be a bit boring from time to time," she said.

"So what are you doing here?" she asked Jake.

"We have this coming week off. I wanted to get to know Selene a little better and she offered to let me crash at her place. Also I don't like my home all that much so I try to spend time with friends over breaks," he said. Just then Alice's mom walked out with a steaming plate of food.

"Dinner is served," Alice's mom said as she set it on the table.

Dinner was delicious. I enjoyed all the homemade food and relaxing conversation.

After dessert I said we had to leave. I was worried about Isaac.

"Thank you for your hospitality," Jake said.

"Thank you for dinner," I said.

"Any time dearies," Alice's mom replied. Jake walked out the door and Alice's mom pulled me over to her.

"He's a good guy—don't lose him," she said. I followed Jake and we went back to my home. Isaac was awake and chewing on my bedpost. I quickly scooped him up into my arms.

"Food," he moaned in my mind. I found the bag Dean Autumn had given us and saw what looked like flower bulbs. I recalled my memory of what dragons were supposed to eat and it looked close enough to the diagram, so I gave three to Isaac. He gulped one down without a blink, then chewed through the second one slower, and just played with the third one before I took it from him and placed it back into the bag. I got undressed and changed into my pjs. Then I went back into the living room. Jake was sitting there just staring off into space in his pjs.

"Are you okay?" I asked and he shook his head, clearing it.

"Yeah I'm fine—just thinking," he said.

"What are you thinking about?" I asked.

"Well if the war never ended, does that mean everything we're learning in school is just to prepare us for all out war?" he asked.

"It may be, but we won't know until it happens," I said.

"But if we do go to war, you will be leading the charge. It's what they want. I'm willing to bet that once Isaac is old enough, they'll declare war," He said.

"It's very likely, but if they make students fight, at least I know you'll have my back," I said.

"Yeah," he sighed.

"You want to see something?" I said.

"Depends what it is," he said.

"Best if you're surprised," I said and pulled him up the hatch that led to the roof. There was a platform with a trunk on it filled with blankets and pillows.

"What is this?" Jake asked.

"It's my stargazing platform. On nights when I can't sleep I look up at the stars," I said.

"But the trees are blocking the sky," he said confused.

"Just wait," I said and went over to the trunk and pulled out the ground blanket that I laid on the platform. I then grabbed some pillows and blankets and threw them on top of the ground blanket. I gestured to Jake and he came over.

"Make yourself comfortable," I said. He grabbed a few pillows and blankets and arranged them to his liking and laid down. I did the same. Then I sent my magic into the trees over my head and bent them apart from each other.

"Whoa," Jake said as the trees revealed the brilliant night sky full of stars. I let the trees get into the new positions and let go of them. They remained in the places I had put them. I gazed up at the stars and sighed.

"I've never seen so many stars before," he said.

"Well if you live near a city or in a place with lots of light, you can't see the stars all that much. But out here you can see everything," I said. A shooting star passed overhead.

"Make a wish," I told him. Jake closed his eyes and then opened them again.

"What did you wish for?" I asked softly.

"If I told you, it wouldn't come true and I really want this wish to come true," he said and looked over at me and smiled. I smiled back and thought to Isaac to come up and join us. Soon his little head was popping up the trap door and he came scampering over the roof and cuddled up beside me. I took one last look at the stars and fell fast asleep.

Chapter 34
IRENE

I woke up Saturday evening to silence. Everything was quiet. I got up and saw that it was almost dinner. I decided to take a shower to shake off my grogginess and then got dressed. I walked into the common room and saw Selene's door open. I peered in and saw the room stripped of everything. I burst in and searched the room. Everything was gone. I ran back into the common room and saw a note on the table.

Dear Irene,

I am leaving. I don't know when I'll come back or if I will come back. This place is not where I belong.

Until next time,
Selene

She left. Why did she leave? So many thoughts were going through my mind. I ran off quickly to Dean Autumn's office.

I arrived and knocked on the door. A "come in" came from within and I opened the door. She was sitting at her desk facing me.

"Irene dear what a surprise! Sit down. Would you like any tea?" she offered as she had done every time I'd ever entered her office before. She was a good friend of my father's so I had been in her office many times.

"No thank you, I came to show you this," I said and handed her the note.

"Ah, yes. I already know about that. I met them leaving the dorm and I stopped them," she said.

"Them?" I questioned.

"Yes Selene and Jake Morales. Weren't you two dating at one point?" she said.

"Where did they go?" I asked her, ignoring her comment.

"I assume she went home. I tried to stop her, but there was no changing her mind. I gave them a week off to think things over and then come back," she said.

"So, she'll come back?" I asked.

"Hopefully. Why do you care about this girl so much?" she asked.

"She's the first person who ever treated me like a normal person. Not like a princess or an object. She's the only one that's been real with me," I told her.

"Ah, I understand. Well would you look at the time. Why don't you go get some dinner? You'll feel better after," she said and I turned and left.

SELENE

The sun shone on my face. It was warm and bright. I moved the trees back into place and the shade covered my eyes. Isaac stirred but stayed asleep. I let him be and looked around. Jake was gone. I got up and put away the blankets and pillows. I left the ground blanket for Isaac to sleep on and went down into the house. Jake was sitting in the dining room eating an apple.

"Morning," I said. He jumped up a little and turned.

"Morning," he replied and continued munching on his apple.

"Is that all you've eaten?" I asked.

"Yeah," he replied.

"How about if I make breakfast?" I asked.

"Sounds good," he said and continued munching on his apple. He seemed in a somber mood. I put some eggs and bacon on the stove and lit the fire. I listened to them start to simmer and sat next to Jake. I stared at him, but he somehow just looked off.

"What's wrong?" I asked him.

"Nothing," he replied and gave me a fake smile.

"Something is obviously bothering you," I said.

"Yeah, there is. I've been going over what you said about what the council did to you," Jake said. I shuddered at the thought.

"I just can't imagine them doing something like that," he said, "Both my parents are on the council. They wouldn't stand for it."

"Maybe they weren't there," I said reassuringly.

"Either way I have questions for them," he said, "I hate to leave you, but I need answers."

"I'll come with you then," I said.

"Really?" he asked.

"Of course. Besides, as much as I love it here, I've lived here my entire life. It's about time I saw some of the world," I said.

"Great! Shall we leave after breakfast?" he asked.

"Sounds good," I replied and tended to the food.

Chapter 35

I said goodbye to Alice and her family as we headed out. Our things were in the back and Isaac was on my lap once again. We drove for about an hour or so and stopped at a McDonald's for lunch, then continued driving. By late afternoon, we drove up to a lavish mansion. Jake pulled into the driveway past a golden gate and pulled up to the front doors. A man came out of the house as Jake and I got out. I hid Isaac under my cloak.

"Christopher, can you park the car in the garage and bring up our bags and prepare a room for my friend here?" Jake said.

"Of course master Jake," he said and bowed. He took the car keys from Jake and drove the car away. Jake walked up to the front doors and motioned for me to follow him. I walked up behind him and as we stepped on the last step the doors opened and we walked inside. Then they closed behind us.

"I'm not going to bother giving you a tour because it would take forever. Literally it takes two hours," he said. I laughed.

"This place is amazing," I said looking around. It's how I would imagine a palace looking from one of my books. Isaac poked his head out from underneath my cloak. I pushed him back underneath not wanting anyone to see him. A door on the side of the room opened and a maid came out.

"Isabelle, are my parents home yet?" Jake asked, "I'd like them to meet a friend."

"Not yet Master Jake, but I will let you know when they are," she said politely.

"Anything I can get you Miss?" she said to me.

"No thank you ma'am," I said politely.

"Anything else for you, Master Jake?" she asked.

"I'm fine, Isabelle, thank you," he said and she walked back through the doors and closed them behind her.

"You want to see the game room?" Jake asked excitedly.

"Sure," I shrugged. I had never been in a game room. Jake took my hand and pulled me up the stairs and turned left. We walked on for a while down a really long hallway and passed a series of identical doors. Finally we stopped near the end of the hallway and Jake opened up the door to the right. Inside was a huge TV with a big sofa in front. A bookcase full of video games stood in the corner. Behind the couch there was a foosball table, a pool table, and a mini arcade arena.

"Whoa!" I said. I had never seen so many games in one place, well except at school.

"So what do you want to do first?" he asked.

"I don't know. It's all so overwhelming," I said staring at the expanse of entertainment.

"Well why don't we start with what you know how to play?" he said.

"I've never played any video or arcade games. I do know how to play pool and foosball though," I said even though most of my knowledge was from what I read in books.

"Great—which one do you want to play?" he asked.

"Let's play pool. I know it better than foosball," I said and walked over to where the cue sticks were. Isaac jumped out from under my cloak and ran across the ground and plopped onto a couch pillow. Jake came up behind me and stared at Isaac.

"Why can't he fly?" he asked and grabbed a cue stick.

"It said in the book that baby dragons can't fly until they are older. At least a week or two," I replied and grabbed a cue stick.

"That makes sense I guess. Do you want to break?" he asked.

"Sure," I replied and I broke causing two of the striped balls to fall into pockets.

"Wow—you're good!" Jake said.

"I used to play something like this back home with stones and sticks," I said and sank another ball.

"So your parents won't mind that you're here and not a school?" I questioned and lined up for another ball.

"They probably will, but I'll just tell them I'm staying for the weekend," he said.

"And they won't mind that I'm here?" I said and hit the ball. It went off to the left and just missed the pocket.

"They might, but you're my guest so they'll have to put up with it," he said and maneuvered to shoot a ball.

"Sounds good," I said and watched him sink the ball.

We played two more games when Isabelle came in.

"Your parents are home, Master Jake. They are waiting for you in the study," Isabelle said.

"Thank you, Isabelle," Jake said and put his cue back on the rack. "Come on, best not to make them wait," he said. I put my cue back on the rack and Isabelle left.

I called Isaac, who picked his head up and scampered over to me and climbed up to his usual perch. I followed Jake out the door and back down the hall. We passed at the stairs and turned down a side hall. At the end were two doors which Jake pushed through. Inside were two large desks and a sitting area. Covering every wall were bookshelves full of books. A man and woman were seated in the sitting area and looked up as Jake and I came in. I hid in the shadow of the doorway as Jake walked up to them.

"Ah, there you are son," said the man who I assumed was Jake's father.

"It's nice to see you," said the woman who must have been Jake's mother. She stood up and gave Jake a hug.

"What brings you here?" Mr. Morales asked.

"Well I wanted to speak with you," Jake said and motioned for me. I walked over and stood next to him.

"What are you doing with this girl, Jake?" Mrs. Morales cried out.

"She's my friend mother," Jake retorted.

"No—she is a danger to mages! She injured four of our best guards and nearly killed the council's mentalist representative." Mr. Morales yelled at him.

"No, they attacked me after I was kidnapped and I was defending myself." I yelled at them. I started to move towards them but Jake held me back.

"Kidnapped? You were brought to us so we could see who you were and if you were a threat to us. The council is deciding this now and so far it looks like you are a threat." Mr. Morales retorted.

"That is a lie you were told! I was taken by force by Dean Autumn and chained up to be brought to you against my will. I was shown like a show pony and then I was abused by your great mentalist. I would call that kidnapping and abuse," I shouted.

Mr. Morales looked at me and stared. We remained silent for a few minutes.

"We had no idea what you went through," Mrs. Morales said quietly.

"Yes, but you were in a safe place. The council would never hurt a possible champion," Mr. Morales said.

"But they did! They entered my mind without my permission and there are things...there are things I don't like people to know," I sighed. Jake hugged me and I looked out from his arms. His parents were looking at us and then looked at each other.

"I think we understand a little better," Mr. Morales said quietly. "So I will let you stay at my home as a guest, but I can't do anything against the council's wishes."

"Thank you. I understand your position," I said and came out from Jake's embrace.

"Yes, now if you don't mind I have never before seen a dragon. May I see yours?" Mrs. Morales asked. I let Isaac out from under my cloak and he scampered around and jumped onto Mrs. Morales shoulder.

Chapter 36
Dean Autumn

"You are here for one reason and that is to watch the school while I'm gone," I said and looked the assistant principal in the eyes.

"Yes ma'am," she said fearfully.

"I should be back by tomorrow at the latest," I said and turned and went through the secret door. I walked into the hallway ignoring the large doors at the end and went into one of the secret side doors. I walked down the long hallway and entered the archives. Here records were kept of every family that had even an ounce of magic in their bloodline. I walked past the workers, daily keeping up the records, and headed towards the back to the dead family lines. These were families that had run out of heirs and the family line had died out. I looked around the shelves hoping not to see member Hunter here as well. I reached the M's and paid more attention to the names.

"Magik, Mick, Moland, Murbell, ah Mystic," I mumbled. Many years ago we had paid our respects to the Mystic family records when it had turned gray and lost its magic. This meant the family line had died out. I opened the scroll and saw the last two Mystics: Isaac and Isabelle Mystic both had frowns in their pictures. Isabelle had been my roommate in school here. She was a blast—we had gotten into so much mischief. I sighed. I really missed her. It had been hard to hear about their deaths.

Isaac was a good man too. I didn't know him that well but Isabelle had loved him ever since she had spotted him in her first class at school. Isabelle had belonged to another powerful mage family, so the possibility of two powerful mage families coming together to have a child was incredible. That child would have the powers of both sides of the family. I looked below their images and saw nothing.

"Mark must have been wrong," I thought. I touched Isabelle's picture as a goodbye and went to roll up the scroll. A piece of paper fell out from the middle.

I bent down to pick it up. There were only a few words:

Rest of records moved to
The Woods family

I stared in shock. The records had never done this before. I made my way to the living records and found the Woods family records. It was just one sheet of paper with one person.

Name: Selene Woods
Formerly known as: Jane Mystic

I stared in shock. Mark was right. Selene was the lost heir to the Mystic family. I looked at the picture and saw that indeed it was Selene, a sad one, but none the less her. I quickly put the paper back and returned to my office with this information in my mind.

SELENE

A hot blast of air woke me up thanks to Isaac snoring next to me. I patted his head and got up. The room I was in was fit for a princess. It was pink with lots of gold accents and a canopy bed. A huge bathroom and closet led off from the main room. I walked past the bathroom door and went to the balcony. Pulling back the pink curtains, I opened the French doors and stepped out into the moonlight, leaning against the balcony. It looked out over the garden and pool in the backyard. I could see the woods behind it and the city lights off in the distance. The moon reflected in the pool and a soft, cool breeze blew by rippling the water. I looked to the side and saw someone else on a balcony to my left, leaning on the railing just as I was. I knew it was Jake. The servants slept on the first floor and his parents' rooms were to my right and no one else lived here. I levitated myself over to him and landed quietly behind him. I walked up beside him and leaned on the railing. We watched the night, taking in all the sights, feeling peaceful. I looked up and saw some stars, but nothing like back home. I looked back to the sight out in front of me.

"I'm sorry about my parents," he said quietly, "They shouldn't have done that."

"It's okay. I understand where they are coming from," I said.

"But it isn't okay," he said and turned to me. I looked at him, the moonlight shining in his eyes.

"Why is this okay for you when it clearly isn't?" he asked.

"I could let it bother me," I said looking out into the world in front of me, "But then I'd be bothered and slowly everything would bother me and I'd lose my peace inside. The war would be waged on my emotions and my fire would consume me, or worse." Jake didn't answer and turned back to the view. I looked at it too and saw a train slowly making its way over a hill, smoke spilling from its funnel.

"Why are you awake?" I asked him.

"Couldn't sleep," he said.

"Bad dreams?" I asked.

"Of sorts. Do you know how my family got ahead of everyone in life?" he asked.

"No," I said.

"Long ago our ancestors helped out a seer. She granted my family the ability to see the future but it's usually just random junk. It gets passed down through every generation but it gets weaker and weaker. My father has it. He must have seen something in the study—something so big that he let you stay here. That worries me," he said.

"Why?" I asked.

"Well it normally isn't good," he said.

"Oh," I said, "Do you get visions?"

"Not yet, but soon," he said.

"When will you get them?"

"It's different for everyone, but I have a feeling about when mine will come," he said and smiled at me. I smiled back and then got a sense of what was to come.

"We should get some sleep," I said. His smile faded.

"Yeah, you're probably right. Goodnight Selene," he said and turned to go inside. I watched him go and something came over me. I ran up behind him and gave him a quick kiss on the cheek and quickly turned, running, and leaped off the balcony, flying back to my room. I looked back and saw Jake watching me go with a hand to where I had kissed him. I landed and went inside and closed the doors. I climbed back into bed and tried to sleep wondering what had come over me.

Chapter 37

We spent the rest of the week at Jake's house. We did some swimming in the indoor pool, played lots of games, and I even played my first video game. The week was soon up and I had almost forgotten about what had happened last Saturday. I was in my room packing up my bag when there was a knock on my door. I went to open it and saw Mrs. Morales.

"Yes ma'am, can I help you?" I asked politely.

"May I come in?" she requested.

"Of course," I replied. She walked in and I closed the door behind her.

"I just wanted to say goodbye. We had a great time hosting you and I'm sorry about the way we started," she said.

"It's okay—I understand. How could you have known what I had been through?" I replied.

"No, no, it wasn't okay. But I've gotten to know you a little better and I'd like to give you a parting gift," she said and presented me with a small box.

"Oh wow—you don't have to give me anything," I said.

"I know, but I want you to have it anyway," she said and pressed it into my hand. I stared at the box in my hand.

"Well, open it," she said. I sat on one of the chairs in the corner and opened up the box. Inside was a beautiful ring. It was silver with the image of a dragon wrapped around the band with its wings folded. Its eyes were small white crystals.

"Oh, it's beautiful! You really don't mind parting with it?" I asked looking up at her.

"I want you to have this. Please take it," she said. "It was my grandmother's. She was great friends with Alfred Anorak's grandson. He was old and had no heirs to his family, so when he died, his will stated that the ring was to be left with my grandmother. When the ring came, a note was left with it. It said to pass it down through our family until the next dragon owner was known. Then we were to give it to them," she said.

"Wow," I sighed.

"I don't know what it will do for you, but I think you are meant to have it," she said, putting her hand on my shoulder.

"Thank you," I said and placed the ring on my ungloved hand.

"I've been meaning to ask. Why are you wearing only one glove?" she questioned. I removed my glove and showed her the mark.

"Oh, it's beautiful. Why do you cover it up?" she asked.

"I don't want to show everyone—you know," I said.

"Oh, yes, of course. I wasn't thinking. Well I'd better leave you to finish packing. Goodbye dear. Goodbye Isaac," she said and left.

I stared at the ring a little longer. "Isaac come and see her gift," I thought to him. He lazily sat up and bounded over, climbed up my shoulder, and looked at the ring.

"It's time mistress," he said and blew fire on my left hand. It was a white fire with hints of blue.

"Isaac—since when could you breathe fire!" I thought frantically.

"I told you the time was right," he said and stopped. I thought the ring would be nothing but a puddle of metal, but to my surprise it wasn't. The dragon on the ring now had its wings spread and fire shaped metal was coming out of its mouth. The crystal eyes were now blue and the whole body was now almost white.

"What did you do?" I asked Isaac, admiring the ring.

"When I saw that ring it meant that it was time to breathe fire. It signified the first breath of fire," he thought to me. I pulled him into a little hug.

"You amaze me every day," I thought to him. I let him go and he climbed back onto the bed.

"When will you be able to fly?" I thought to him as I resumed packing.

"When the next time is right," he said and went to sleep.

"Of course," I thought.

I finished packing and met Jake in the hall. Isaac was asleep on my shoulders letting out some small snores here and there.

"Ready to go?" he asked.

"As ready as I'll ever be," I replied and we walked outside. Jake's car was waiting for us. Christopher handed Jake his keys with a farewell. We got into the car and drove away.

It was a few hours' drive from his house, but the trip flew by and we were soon driving to the school parking lot. We got out and

I grabbed my bag. Jake grabbed his, made sure his car was locked, and then we went into the school. As we reached the elevator Jake turned to me.

"I have to go to my dorm," he said. "My roommate has probably been wondering where I am."

"That's fine. Thank you for coming with me," I said.

"No problem," he said. The elevator opened and he got in. I waited for another elevator and looked around the main hall, remembering the first time I laid eyes on it. The doors opened and I stepped in, pressing in the code for my dorm. The doors closed and I went up.

I walked out of the elevator and opened the door to the dorm. Irene was at the table eating an apple. She heard the door open and looked up.

"Selene, I'm so glad you're back," she said, getting up and hugging me.

"It's good to see you too Irene," I said and hugged her back.

"Well I'll let you get settled. How is Isaac?" she asked. At the sound of his name, Isaac poked his head out from my cloak.

"Go and play with Irene," I thought to him. He jumped off my shoulder and onto Irene's.

"Can you watch him for me?" I asked.

"Of course," she said and tickled Isaac under his chin. I smiled and went into my dorm room. I set my bag down and let my things find their places. I sat down next to the window and looked out into the world. I heard voices in the common room and then there was a knock on my door. I opened it to see Dean Autumn's assistant.

"You are to report to Dean Autumn's office," she said and then left. I watched her go and just stared into space. I didn't want to go. Last time I was there I had been kidnapped. Irene saw that I was worried.

"What's wrong?" she asked.

"Nothing important. Watch Isaac for me while I'm gone," I said.

"Take me with you," Isaac cried to my thoughts.

"I don't want what happened last time to happen again. You'll be safer here," I told him and left for Dean Autumn's office.

Chapter 38

I walked out of the elevator to the door of her office. I was nervous and I didn't know what to expect, so I prepared myself just in case I was attacked. I took the necklace I had made and put in my hand to form it into a dagger. I knocked on the door and heard Dean Autumn say, "Come in." I opened the door and stepped inside. She was sitting where she always did at her desk.

"Please have a seat Jane," she said. I remained standing and stared at her.

"What did you just call me?" I asked threateningly.

"Jane," she said again.

"Where did you get that name?" I asked angrily.

"It's yours so why should it matter," she said. I took out the dagger and pointed it at her.

"Where. Did. You. Get. That. Name?" I asked again.

"Okay, okay," she said, realizing this wasn't a game anymore.

"From the archives. They keep the history of all mage families," she said quickly. I lowered my knife and just stared at her.

"So are you Jane Mystic?" she asked. I stayed silent for a while and then answered her.

"I haven't been her since she let her emotions take over eleven years ago. She couldn't handle her emotions so I shut her away," I said. A pain shot through the side of my head like a lightning bolt making me wince.

"So what happened to you—I mean her?" she asked.

"I buried her in my mind and hid all her painful memories. I only kept one to remind me why I am like this—why I did this," I said and turned away.

"So is Jane dead?" she asked.

"Why do you care so much?" I yelled, turning back to face Dean Autumn.

"Isabelle, your mother, was a great friend of mine," she said slowly. I stared at her in shock—she had known my mother.

"I thought that Jane might have been more like her," she said.

"I don't know if Jane is dead, but if she isn't, she hides away where she belongs—in her memories," I said. My head was still hurting.

"Can she be brought back?" she asked.

"I will not allow it," I said and threw my knife just over Dean Autumn's head. "Don't call me Jane again or the next time my dagger will be in your skull," I said leaning towards her and grabbing the dagger. I formed it back into the necklace and left.

I walked back into the dorm and breezed by Irene and went into my room slamming the door. My head hurt a lot and I was getting angry for the first time since the accident. I paced my room thinking and thinking, but it only got worse and my head hurt more and more.

"Isaac," I thought, "Get Irene out of here."

"Yes mistress," he said sensing my distress. My head started to hurt more and I was angry and something in me was suddenly afraid and another part was almost happy. I went to the wall and punched it, but it didn't help. Then everything came exploding out. Fire surrounded me with a roaring passion. I couldn't control it.

"Selene, let me back in," a little girl's voice called out. It was Jane—the old me—the person who felt emotion. I knew deep down that she had something to do with the death of my parents.

"Never—you bring pain and sorrow. You somehow killed them," I called out.

"But I am you and you are incomplete without me. I didn't do anything. You just need someone to blame" the voice said.

"I don't want to be completed by you and I know it was you," I said.

"But you will be more in control of your actions if we are complete," Jane said. And then she whispered as if right next to my ear, "You will be more powerful with both our magics combined. You could defeat anyone that bothers you. We would be unstoppable. You would never lose control again—never accidentally hurt anyone." She showed me the memory of what the council had done to me, then showed me a vision of me defeating them all without her accidentally killing anyone. Then she showed me with her living a long happy life with my friends. I thought about it for a second and she took her chance. She broke out of her memory prison and into my side of our mind. I felt as if my mind would rip apart.

"Stop," I shouted and the roaring sound ceased, but the fire remained.

"Why did you do this to me? We were happy, powerful, and one," she called.

"You were hurting people and it wasn't helping either of us. You were emotionally weak," I said.

"But I didn't do anything. You blamed me for something I never did and your emotions don't make you weak—they make you strong," she said.

"I know that now. Back then I thought it was the right choice to hide you away. I am willing to undo my actions now though," I said.

"So I can take over?" she said happily.

"No, but we can be one again if I am in control. We can be strong once again, but you cannot be in control. I'm not ready for that," I said.

"I'll take what I can get. You will learn to be one with me," she said and the fire slowly died down. The pain in my head ceased and I felt better inside and could feel that my soul was more complete. I was me again—the old me. With the flames gone I saw the damage I had caused. Everything was burnt. The window and door had been blown out and part of the common room was scorched. I sighed and started a repair spell that would turn everything back to normal. The window was replaced as well as the door. My books and bookshelf slowly remade themselves and the bed as well. My desk started growing back as well as my window seat. The paint came back and the scorch marks disappeared. I sat in the window area and stared out the window again.

"Why did she have to mention Jane?" I thought.

"Because it was time," Jane answered.

"Isaac bring Irene back please," I thought to him.

"Yes mistress—who else is in your head?" he asked.

"My old self, but pay no attention to her," I thought.

"Hey!" Jane said. I walked into the common room and saw Isaac run back in with one of Irene's favorite shoes.

"Get back here Isaac," she shouted, "Selene can you help me here?" Isaac jumped up to his usual perch and dropped the shoe in my hand.

"Here Irene," I said, handing her the shoe.

"Little trickster," she directed at Isaac.

"Good work, but don't do it again," I thought to Isaac.

"What happened here?" Irene asked as the last of the scorch marks disappeared.

"I made a mess and had to clean it up," I said. Then there was a banging on the door. Irene opened it and none other than Dean Autumn was in the doorway.

"I got reports that there was a fire here," she said calmly.

"Yeah, no thanks to you," I said and slumped onto the couch.

"I only did what I thought was best," she said.

"Best for who," I replied. Silence followed from her.

"I'm confused," Irene said.

"I'll tell you later. Can you please give Dean Autumn and I some privacy," I said.

"Fine," she replied and stomped off into her room and closed the door with a slam. Dean Autumn walked in and sat next to me.

"Listen, I know you don't want to hear this, but being a Mystic means that you may have more power than you know," she said.

"I know, but not right now. I need time to think," I said.

"I understand," she said, "One last question, which name would you like to go by?" I thought for a minute but didn't answer.

"I'll let you think it over," she said and stood up. She walked across to me and gave me a hug.

"You look just like your mother," she said and left. I sat there for a few minutes watching the fire burn away the wood logs in the fireplace.

Chapter 39

Night fell and I was sitting in my room talking with Jane.

"I don't like having another voice in my head. It's just strange," I said.

"I know but I can't be quiet. I had to be for so long and now all I want to do is talk," she squealed.

"Maybe we should become more together. Not quite one person but enough that I don't have to hear your voice all the time," I said, "Those years were the best, I must admit. We were happy, but you hurt people, so we can't be fully together."

"Yes, they were good years. I didn't cause Mom and Dad to die. Something else happened that night. We just had bad luck with timing on our part," she said and in my mind she slowly walked up to me.

"You really had no involvement?" I asked. She looked at me and shook her head no.

"I swear," she said. I took her hand in mine.

"Then what happened?" I asked.

"I don't know, but we'll figure it out together," she said. I smiled and nodded at her.

"Ready?" she asked.

"I trust you. I'm ready to be together again," I said. I felt our minds meld and it felt as if I had another personality. We weren't fighting for control and neither one of us was being shut away.

"Thank you," she said softly and then her voice went silent. All of the painful memories from my past came rushing back to me, but I had it under control. It was good to have the memories back with the full emotion. I could feel again and it wasn't bad at all.

If my emotions were no longer bottled up, could I still make fire? I had to try. I focused on my fire with Jane's mind slipping into mine, and as one, a small flame appeared in the palm of my hand. I was slightly surprised. Without the fuel of pent up emotions for my fire to burn I would have thought it would no longer work.

Something in me made me realize that the hadn't been from my hidden emotions at all. I had been born with this fire. I looked around the room with new eyes and a new, complete soul. I thought back to Dean Autumn's question from earlier. What was my name?

Should I go back to being Jane and was I even a Mystic? I thought about it some more and decided. Suddenly my stomach let out a rumble and I looked at the clock seeing it was almost eight o'clock. I walked out of the dorm down to the dining hall.

"Hey! You're back. We missed you," Sarah said when I sat down at the table across from her and Noah and next to Jake.

"Me too," I replied.

"Yeah it's been a bit boring this week without you two," Noah said to Jake and I.

"Hey," Sarah said, elbowing him in the side.

"Not that I haven't had a great time with you my love," he added sheepishly.

"That's better," Sarah said, pecking his lips.

"So I was thinking in celebration of your return, we have a great night at the Cavern," he said.

"Ooh, fun," Sarah said.

"I'm down. How about you Selene?" Jake asked.

"I have something to take care of first, but after that I'm free to join in," I said.

"Great! Meet me in the library when you're all ready," Noah said and I started digging into my food.

I knocked on the door and heard the usual, "Come in." I opened the office door and Dean Autumn looked up.

"I've chosen my name," I said.

"Oh, good," she replied and I sat down in front of her desk.

"I'm not Jane," I told her and her face fell, "but I am a Mystic."

"So?" she questioned.

"So, my name will now be Selene Mystic," I replied.

"I think you made a good choice dear. Your mother would be

very proud of you," she said, "Now go have some fun with your friends."

I smiled and left.

DEAN AUTUMN

I walked out of the secret door and into the archives. I passed through the empty working areas and went to the location where Selene Wood's file was. As I reached it I saw that it had grayed and faded. I picked it up and placed it in the dead records area, making certain I was placing it in the correct location. I went over to the Mystic family file and saw that the color was already returning to it. I opened it and saw Selene's name with her proper family name listed below Isaac and Isabelle. I smiled and picked up the scroll happily. I carried it to the living records and placed it happily into the correct location. I looked above Selene's picture and saw Isabelle and Isaac with smiles on their faces looking at Selene's picture lovingly. I left knowing that everything was alright for now.

SELENE

I pushed open the doors to the library seeing my friends sitting at a table.

"Can I help you?" the librarian asked.

"No thank you ma'am. I'm just meeting up with some friends," I said. She just looked at me and rolled her eyes returning to the stack of books in front of her.

"So is everyone ready to party?" Noah asked.

"Almost. I want to tell you all something," I said. "Due to recent events, things have changed for me. I thought it was only right for you all to know my real name." They all stared at me.

"My real name is Jane Mystic," I said. There was silence then a squeal from Sarah.

"You're from the Mystic family. It was one of the most powerful families that died out over ten years ago—that Mystic family!" Sarah repeated.

"Yes, but I'm still going to go by Selene. Jane is someone different from who I am now. I may be more like her, but I'm not her," I replied.

"Selene Mystic," Jake said, "I like it. It has a nice ring to it." He came over to me and gave me a shoulder hug.

"So let's go party!" I exclaimed. Noah led the way, map in hand. We walked down side halls and went into tonight's location for the Cavern. Sarah and Noah went over to the drink station.

"What do you want to do?" I asked Jake.

"How about we go for a swim? I know how much you like the water," he offered. I nodded in agreement and we made our way over to the locker rooms.

I came out of the locker rooms in a two piece gray suit. Jake was waiting for me by the door wearing a pair of black swim trunks. I realized that this was the first time I had seen him with his shirt off. I couldn't help but stare at his muscular figure.

"Something you like?" he chuckled.

"Maybe," I said. Then I caught him looking me over.

"Something you like?" I teased back at him.

"There's nothing about you I don't like," he said, stepping closer to me. When he was right in front of me I stepped closer to him and leaned in so my mouth was right next to his ear.

"Race you," I whispered and I pushed off him and ran to the pool. He ran after me and tried to catch me, but I was too quick. I dove into the pool and came up as he reached the pool and jumped in splashing me. He came back up to the surface and I splashed him in return. We both laughed and swam out into the deeper water to get away from everyone.

"I want to show you something," he said and took my hand. He pulled me over to a secret grotto that I had never noticed before now.

JAKE

I took Selene's hand and led her to the secret grotto I had found on one of my other visits to the Cavern. I pulled her into the shallow end and we both stood up. I pulled her over to the rock ledge that was made as a bench. She sat next to me and placed her hand on mine. Something had changed in her. She seems to be more herself and not the closed-off girl I first met. That hadn't changed the way I felt about her though. Her eyes were sparkling with the light from the gems in the walls. I wanted nothing more than to kiss her here and now. She was the most beautiful girl in the world and I wanted to treat her like a queen. I wish she would take up my offer for a date soon....Suddenly she smiled shyly.

"What are you thinking?" I asked.

"Jake, I'm going to take you up on that date," she said. My heart jumped in my chest and I could barely believe what I had heard.

"Really?" I said. I was so excited.

"Yes. I want to be with you," she said. My heart started beating faster and I've never felt so happy.

"I have waited too long for you to say those words," I said quietly. I moved a stray piece of hair away from her face and put it behind her ear. I leaned in closer to her and put my hand on the side of her face.

SELENE

He pulled me into the shallow end of the grotto and we stood up facing each other. He pulled me over to a rock ledge that had been carved out, most likely by magic, to make a bench. We took a seat next to each and I placed my hand on his. I turned and looked at Jake with his eyes reflecting the light of the glowing crystals around us. He looked at me lovingly and I thought back to his offer about going on a date. I smiled at the thought. Suddenly a mischievous smile broke across his face.

"What are you thinking?" he asked.

"Jake, I'm going to take you up on that date," I said.

"Really?" he said quickly. He acted like an excited puppy.

"Yes. I want to be with you," I said, my heart pounding in my chest.

"I've waited too long for you to say those words," he said quietly. He leaned in and put a piece of my hair behind my ear. His hand came to rest on the side of my face. I stared into his eyes and he leaned in closer. I closed my eyes and felt his lips touch mine and we shared a kiss. I had never experienced something that felt this good. It made me feel warm and fuzzy and I never wanted it to end. I couldn't help but smile into the kiss. When we parted we looked into each other's eyes. I saw nothing but love in his. He smiled at me as I wrapped my hands around his neck and then I pulled him back to my lips. We parted again a few seconds later and sat next to each other again. I leaned my head on his shoulders enjoying hearing his heartbeat as he laid his head on mine. Soon we heard our names being called by our friends and we swam back to shore ending our perfect time with each other.

I lay in bed that night, tucked snuggly under my covers, staring at the ceiling. Isaac was asleep on my stomach, snoring lightly with his fire radiating warmth through the room. I patted his back softly so that I wouldn't wake him. I closed my eyes and remembered my kiss with Jake and all the other perfect moments that had happened since I came here. I sighed in happiness.

"This won't last forever you know. Things are going to change," Jane whispered as I drifted off to sleep.

About The Author

Eclipsa Moon was born and raised in New Milford, Connecticut, where she currently lives with her parents. A full-time student, she spends her free time reading, painting, and playing RPG games. Through these games, she discovered her love for writing and was inspired to write "The  Dragon's Mark." You can follow her and keep up with her future works on Instagram @eclipsa.moon_

CPSIA information can be obtained
at www.ICGtesting.com
Printed in the USA
BVHW040221220121
598405BV00017B/644